THE O'DOOLES
OF RESEDA

THE O'DOOLES OF RESEDA

A YEAR IN THE LIFE OF AMERICA'S MOST DYSFUNCTIONAL FAMILY

Tim Ballou and Linda Higgins

A Citadel Press Book
Published by Carol Publishing Group

A Citadel Press Book.
Published by Carol Publishing Group
Citadel Press is a registered trademark of Carol Communications, Inc.
Editorial Offices: 600 Madison Avenue, New York, N.Y. 10022
Sales and Distribution Offices: 120 Enterprise Avenue, Secaucus, N.J.
    07094
In Canada: Canadian Manda Group, One Atlantic Avenue, Suite 105,
    Toronto, Ontario M6K 3E7
Queries regarding rights and permissions should be addressed to Carol
    Publishing Group, 600 Madison Avenue, New York, N.Y. 10022

Carol Publishing Group books are available at special discounts for bulk purchases, sales promotion, fund-raising, or educational purposes. Special editions can be created to specifications. For details, contact: Special Sales Department, Carol Publishing Group, 120 Enterprise Avenue, Secaucus, N.J. 07094.

Manufactured in the United States of America
10 9 8 7 6 5 4 3 2 1

Library of Congress Cataloging-in-Publication Data
Ballou, Tim.
    The O'Dooles of Reseda : a year in the life of America's most
dysfunctional family / by Tim Ballou and Linda Higgins.
        p.   cm.
    "A Citadel Press book."
    ISBN 0-8065-1609-7
    I. Higgins, Linda.   II. Title.
PS3552.A47129O36   1995
813'.54—dc20   94-46564
                                                    CIP

INTRODUCTION

The following pages contain correspondence written by and to members of an earnest, hard-working American family who live in the unpretentious Los Angeles, California, suburb called Reseda. They are the O'Dooles, and they are comprised of Atwood, Polly, A.J., Maureen ("Mo"), and Penny.

This book is much more than a random collection of what has passed in and out of the O'Dooles' mailbox. It is every bit as much of a story as *Gone With the Wind,* with a bona fide beginning, middle, and end. To be honest, that's about all it has in common with *Gone With the Wind,* but who says all great literature has to have antebellum mansions and neurotic heroines?

Before you start reading, we feel that we must confess something which may or may not become obvious later on—the O'Dooles do not really exist. We wrote all the letters, postcards, and diary entries ourselves. We even signed their names and licked the stamps. Although the O'Dooles exist in the same dimension as Santa Claus, the Easter Bunny, and Spinal Tap, the people they (we) wrote to and the letters which were written back to us (the O'Dooles) are as authentic as death and taxes.

In closing, we want to thank each and every one of our unknowing collaborators—politicians, actors and actresses, heads of corporations, scientists, lawyers, and a guy named Glondo who makes the best beef jerky in the Northwest. They made this book a lot of fun to write and, we hope, even more fun to read.

Tim Ballou and Linda Higgins

THE O'DOOLES
OF RESEDA

POLLY O'DOOLE
6857 BOTHWELL ROAD
RESEDA, CA   91335

January 8, 1992

Greenpeace
1436 U Street, N.W.
Washington, D.C.   20009
Attn: <u>Ocean Ecology</u>

Dear Madam/Sir:

I just had a thought for a TV commercial that your organization
might be able to use to help those big oil companies stop
polluting our waters. I wrote a song that would have a very
powerful impact if you paired it up with some slides or pictures
that would show just what damage is being done.

I personally made up these lyrics but I think you might have to
get Simon and Garfunkel's approval for using the music. I don't
know about Art Garfunkel, but Paul Simon seems like the type to
be really jazzed about saving the environment.

Please let me know what you decide. I will donate all proceeds
to Greenpeace. If you don't want to use my lyrics, let me know
because maybe another environmental agency would like it even if
you don't. But, I hope you do!

Sincerely,

Polly O'Doole
Polly O'Doole

ARE YOU GOING TO CLEAN UP THIS WATER?
(Sung to the tune of "Are You Going to Scarborough Fair?")
by Paul Simon and Art Garfunkel

Are you going to clean up this water?
Would you serve a glass to your daughter?
Syringes, needles, oil and waste
Do not make for a very good taste

(You could show a glass full of oil and syringes in some
dirty water.)

Are you going to clean up oil spills?
Oil now covers our birds' beaks and bills
We can't eat fish cause oil makes them sicken
Instead of red meat we can only eat chicken

(You could show dead fish and oil covered birds.)

Are you going to clean up our seas?
Can we swim without catching disease?
You might comply if enough people hollar
But do it without spending my tax dollar!

(I can't think of a good picture for this one.)

GREENPEACE

Greenpeace • 1436 U Street NW • Washington DC 20009 •

April 23, 1992

Polly O'Doole
66857 Bothwell Road
Reseda, CA 91335

Dear Ms. O'Doole:

Thank you for thinking of Greenpeace when you wrote your
environmental lyrics to "Are You Going to Scarborough Fair?" Your
dedication and creativity are vital to supporting our work.

Unfortunately, as much as we would like to be able to use your
lyrics, we simply do not, at this time, have a way of using them.
So rather than holding on to them until such a time as we could use
them, I am returning your lyric sheet.

I hope you will continue to pursue other environmental
organizations with your idea as it is possible that one of them is
better equipped to work with you.

Once again, we appreciate your interest in Greenpeace. Please
accept the enclosed stickers as a personal thank you from me.

Peace,

Nadya Labib
Development

POLLY O'DOOLE
6857 BOTHWELL ROAD
RESEDA, CA 91335

January 16, 1992

Governor James Florio
Governor of New Jersey
125 West State Street
CN 001
Trenton, New Jersey 08625

Dear Governor Florio:

On a recent Eye Witness News Program (Channel 7 - ABC) I heard that from now on it is against the law to serve eggs "over easy" in the State of New Jersey. I didn't hear the whole story but I think it had something to do with a type of poison if the eggs aren't cooked properly. I have three children and they like eggs (me too!). I use eggs in lots of different foods. How about when you dip bread into raw eggs to make French toast? My daughter and I sometimes mix up an egg and give each other facials. Is it dangerous to put a raw egg on your face? Can you still serve eggs "over easy" in the privacy of your home or is it still against the law?

I would appreciate it if you could give me some egg guidelines so I can protect my family from "egg"cidental poisoning. I live in California and nobody here told us anything about these eggs. Are there any other kinds of foods or products that are banned in New Jersey that I should be aware of?

Please let me know what's going on and keep up the good work.

Sincerely,

Polly O'Doole

Polly O'Doole

P.S. Are omelettes safe?

State of New Jersey
DEPARTMENT OF HEALTH
CN 360
TRENTON, N.J. 08625-0360

FRANCES J. DUNSTON, M.D., M.P.H.
STATE COMMISSIONER OF HEALTH

March 11, 1992

Ms. Polly O'Doole
6857 Bothwell Road
Reseda, CA 91335

Dear Ms. O'Doole:

Your letter to Governor Florio regarding New Jersey's requirements for the handling and service of eggs in retail food establishments has been referred to this office for reply. I hope that the following information is helpful in answering your inquiry.

Any food which contains raw or undercooked eggs may contain sufficient numbers of the salmonella bacteria to cause disease. Thorough cooking readily destroys the bacteria. Therefore, foods which contain eggs such as french toast and omelettes may be safely served provided they are fully cooked (to a temperature of 140 F) or are made with commercially available pasteurized eggs.

Is it against the law to serve eggs "over easy" in the privacy of your home? No, New Jersey's actions were taken through amending Chapter XII of the State Sanitary Code which is entitled "Sanitation in Retail Food Establishments and Food and Beverage Vending Machines." These rules are enforceable only in retail food establishments in New Jersey.

Is it dangerous to put a raw egg on your face? No, epidemiological evidence indicates that the transmission of Salmonella enteritidis associated with eggs is limited to the consumption of eggs.

The recent attention this issue has received has heightened public awareness of the problem of contaminated eggs and the precautions that can be taken to prevent foodborne illness associated with Salmonella enteritidis . However, it should be noted that the increase in the incidence of Salmonella enteritidis associated with the consumption of undercooked eggs has been reported primarily in the Northeast and the Middle Atlantic States. Therefore, it is recommended that you contact the appropriate health authority in your state for guidance regarding the health risks associated with the consumption of raw or undercooked eggs in your area.

For your information, I have enclosed background information on this issue and guidelines for the safe handling and preparation of eggs.

Thank you for your concern in this matter. If you have any additional questions, please contact me in writing or by telephone.

Sincerely,

William N. Manley
Coordinator, Health Projects
Retail Food
Food and Milk Program

Enclosures

2. Refrigerate eggs at home in their original carton as soon as possible, at a temperature no higher than 40°F. Do not wash eggs before storing or using them. Washing is a routine part of commercial egg processing and rewashing is unnecessary.

3. Use raw shell ~~hard~~

FOR MORE INFORMATION ON HANDLING EGGS SAFELY, CALL USDA'S MEAT AND POULTRY ~~HO~~TLINE: 1-800-535-4555; Washington, D.C. area, call (202) 447-3333. ~~The~~ hours are 10 a.m. to 4 p.m. Eastern Time.

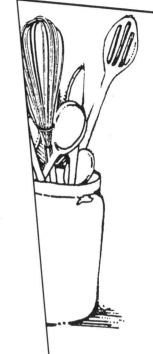

Consumer Bulletin

Handling Eggs Safely at Home

September 1988

United States Department of Agriculture Food and Drug Administration

Raw eggs that were contaminated with Salmonella enteritidis bacteria have caused some recent outbreaks of food-borne illness.

Scientists strongly suspect that Salmonella bacteria can be transmitted from infected laying hens directly into the interior of the eggs before the shells are formed. The full extent of the problem is not yet known, but scientists are working to find solutions.

While the risk of contracting salmonellosis from raw or undercooked eggs is extremely small, eggs are a perishable product and should be treated as such. As with any other perishable food product, proper storage and cooking of eggs is necessary to prevent the growth of potentially harmful bacteria. Consumers should continue to follow safe food-handling practices when preparing eggs.

Special precautions are needed, however, when eggs are served or sold to people in high-risk categories who are particularly vulnerable to Salmonella enteritidis infections: the very young, the elderly, pregnant women (because of risk to the fetus), and people already weakened by serious illness or whose immune systems are weakened.

Consumers should:

1. Avoid eating raw eggs and foods containing raw eggs: Home-made Caesar salad and Hollandaise sauce, for example. Products such as home-made ice cream, home-made eggnog, and home-made mayonnaise should also be avoided, but commercial forms of these products are safe to serve since they are made with pasteurized eggs. Commercial pasteurization destroys Salmonella bacteria.

2. Cook eggs thoroughly until both the yolk and white are firm, not runny, in order to kill any bacteria that may be present. There may be some risk in eating eggs lightly cooked: soft-cooked, soft-scrambled, or sunny-side-up, for example.

3. Realize that eating lightly cooked foods containing eggs, such as soft custards, meringues, and French toast, **may also be risky for people with weakened immune systems and other high-risk groups.**

Consumers should also follow the usual safe food-handling practices for eggs:

1. Use grade AA or A eggs with clean, uncracked shells. It's best if they have been stored under refrigeration.

POLLY O'DOOLE
6857 BOTHWELL ROAD
RESEDA, CA 91335

January 18, 1992

PETA
(People for the Ethical Treatment of Animals)
P.O. Box 42516
Washington, D.C. 20015

Dear Madame/Sir:

My husband, Atwood, and I are very upset with your organization.
Our thirteen year-old daughter, Maureen (Mo), came home from
school crying last week because some children at her school were
making fun of her because she was eating a meat sandwich. They
called her a "cow killer". These same children walked past our
house last week and saw Mo feeding our dog, Earl. They asked her
if she was feeding the dog to "fatten him up" before she killed
him to make hot dogs. When I approached the parents of these
children I was shocked to hear that they share the same opinion
as their bratty kids. They also quoted your organization. Can
you please explain what kind of organization would promote
terrorizing people into not eating meat? I know it's against the
law to serve eggs "over easy" in New Jersey, but as far as I
know, it's not a crime to eat a hamburger in California!

My daughter is now afraid to eat meat in public! And she just
got over the egg thing. She is very mad at your organization and
I encouraged her to vent her anger in a creative way. I am
enclosing a poem that Maureen wrote about her experience with
militant renegade PETA members.

Please, for the sake of the children, don't encourage anti-meat
eating terrorism.

Sincerely,

Polly O'Doole

Polly O'Doole

DON'T YELL AT ME CAUSE I EAT MEAT
by
Maureen (mo) O'Doole

Don't yell at me cause I eat meat
Take a look at your own feet
Do you wear a leather shoe?
If you do, then shame on you!

Leather doesn't come from out of thin air
It's made by removing the cow's underwear
When I eat meat you people curse
But you use a cow's skin as a purse

We all have to answer to God one day
When it's your turn I bet He'll say:
"How come you think you're so Holy?
What did you live on? Guacamole?"

The End

PEOPLE FOR THE ETHICAL
TREATMENT OF ANIMALS
P.O. BOX 42516
WASHINGTON DC
20015-0516

October 15, 1992

Polly O'Doole
6857 Bothwell Rd.
Reseda, CA 91335

Dear Mrs. O'Doole:

Thank you for your letter and for sharing with us the very clever poem by your daughter, Mo. I apologize that you have not received a response sooner, but would like to take this opportunity to address your concerns.

Mo's point about leather is well-taken and here at PETA we urge people to avoid not only leather, but also other animal-derived products such as wool, down, and silk. In addition, members are urged to avoid dairy and egg products because, although animals are not necessarily killed to produce these items, they can suffer greatly in the process.

But we don't expect everyone to become Gandhi overnight. Our job is to simply present people with the facts and let their consciences do the rest. Your conscience might allow you to support industries that inflict tremendous suffering on animals who are equally as sensitive, innocent, and loving as your dog, Earl. Someday, you may come to feel, as we do, that this suffering does not need to be part of your diet; but that is your decision to make when you choose to make it.

Sadly, children can sometimes be cruel and parents can be overly protective. PETA does not condone acts of violence against <u>any living creature</u> (including humans!), but we cannot hope to individually police our more than 350,000 members nationwide. All we can do is apologize on their behalf and hope that you don't judge our cause by the unfortunate acts of a few of its less than sterling representatives.

Thanks again for taking the time to share your concerns.

Sincerely,

Alisa Mullins
Correspondent

My Diary

JANUARY 19, 1992

I feel like I've sold my soul to the devil. The other day at school, some kids were taunting me because I brought a meat sandwich to lunch. After they explained the grizzly details of what that cow went through in order to end up between two slices of bread, I felt sorrier for the cow than for myself. In a rare moment of cameraderie, I shared my new poem "Question For a Carnivor" with mom. Not only did she not "get it", she insisted I only write poems that rhyme. I tried explaining that not all poems rhyme. She replied "All the good ones do!" Just to annoy her, I wrote a rhyming poem that sounds like a 5 year old wrote it -- "Don't Yell at Me Cause I Eat Meat!" She loved it! She mailed it to PETA! I'm just glad she didn't write a song about it. MO

Question For a Carnivor
by Mo O'Doole

As the mutilated piece of flesh travels
past your throat
Down the esophigus and towards its final
resting place within the confines of a
sewer pipe

Ask this question of yourself

How does murder taste?
Is it ummmmm - ummmmm good?

Atwood O'Doole
6857 Bothwell Road
Reseda, California 91335

===

January 20, 1992

Ms. Janine Turner
c/o "Northern Exposure"
3000 Olympic Blvd., #2575
Santa Monica, California 90404

Dear Ms. Turner:

My name is Atwood O'Doole. In addition to owning an awning
and canopy company (O'Doole's Awning & Canopy) I am also your
number one fan. You are my favorite prime time celebrity for the
second year in a row. I have watched almost every episode of
"Northern Exposure". I missed one because my wife Polly made me
watch "Turner and Hooch" on HBO with her. It was stupid. You're
much more talented than Tom Hanks. Or that dog.

I understand that your program is shot on location in
Roslyn, Washington. I've never been to Washington but I've heard
the fishing is great and it rains a lot. I plan on making a trip
to the area this summer with my son A.J. Would you like to go
fishing with us? I haven't found Roslyn on the map yet but I
will and I'm sure there is a nice lake or stream somewhere
nearby. I know you're busy memorizing lines, so I could make
sure to bring extra tackle and snacks for you.

Are Maggie and Dr. Fleischman ever going to actually date
each other? I know it's probably a secret and the producers
don't want you to talk about it but I promise you can trust me.
I would only tell my wife Polly and she doesn't watch your show
anyway. If you want to wait till we go fishing to tell me that's
ok. In the meantime though, can you send me a picture of
yourself?

Very truly yours,

Atwood O'Doole

Atwood O'Doole

Atwood,
Best Wishes,
Janine
Turner

Atwood O'Doole
6857 Bothwell Road
Reseda, California 91335

━━

January 22, 1992

Ms. Gale Thompson
Tourism Program Specialist
Department of Trade and Economic Development
101 General Administration Bldg.
Olympia, Washington 98504-0813

Dear Ms. Thompson:

My name is Atwood O'Doole. In addition to owning an awning
and canopy company (O'Doole's Awning & Canopy) I also love to fish.
Much to my dismay, I have not yet fished in the great state of
Washington. Not yet anyway. I am planning a trip north this
summer and I would like you to send me information about lakes and
streams.

I will be fishing with my pride and joy, A.J., age 15, as well
as Janine ("Northern Exposure") Turner, age unknown. Since
Janine's schedule is so hectic, we'd like to find a place close to
Roslyn, where she works. I don't know where Roslyn is but I am
pretty sure you do. We're also going to need fishing licenses.
Could you tell me who I can contact and how much they are? Are
there any campgrounds in the area? I would like to bring my tent,
which I made myself.

Thank you in advance for your help.

Very truly yours,

Atwood O'Doole

Atwood O'Doole

State of Washington
TRADE & ECONOMIC DEVELOPMENT
General Administration Building, Olympia, WA 98504-0613

OLYMPIA JAN 28 '92 WASH.

U.S. POSTAGE
2.74

PB METER
6745704

THIRD CLASS

Atwood O'Doole
6857 Bothwell Road
Reseda, CA 91335

Washington
A Constant State of Wonder.

Washington

DEPARTMENT OF WILDLIFE
1992-93
GAME FISH REGULATIONS
—pamphlet edition—

Effective from April 16, 1992 to April 15, 1993,
both dates inclusive.

600 CAPITOL WAY N
OLYMPIA, WA 98501-1091

Darrell Pruitt 1992 ©

DESTINATION WASHINGTON®

THE OFFICIAL
WASHINGTON STATE
TRAVELERS' GUIDE™

GTE Discovery Publications, Inc.

Atwood O'Doole
6857 Bothwell Road
Reseda, California 91335

January 23, 1992

Kellogg Company
Consumer Affairs Department
P.O. Box CAMB
Battle Creek, Michigan 49016-1986

Dear Sir/Madam:

My name is Atwood O'Doole. In addition to owning an awning and canopy company (O'Doole's Awning & Canopy) I am also quite an advocate of Corn Flakes. Somehow my morning just isn't complete without a big bowl of Corn Flakes with two spoons of sugar sprinkled on top and my favorite fruit sliced and mixed within. I alternate the fruit -- on Monday and Wednesday I have banana, Tuesday and Thursday I enjoy blueberries, Friday, Saturday and Sunday are strawberry days.

Though my wife Polly does most of the shopping for my family, I have on occasion strolled through our local market too. I am always amazed at the variety of breakfast cereals available to the public. There are fruity cereals, chocolaty cereals, nutty cereals and even cereals shaped like cartoon characters. Amidst all this lies Kellogg's Corn Flakes, as far as I'm concerned the greatest breakfast cereal on the market today. But, you have to admit, to the average shopper Corn Flakes might seem a little bland.

I have an idea. And you can use it free of charge if you want. Frosted Flakes have got Tony the Tiger and his "They're Grrrreat!" shtick, so why shouldn't Corn Flakes have a rep too? First of all, shape all your flakes like little minnows. They'll still taste the same, but they'll look like minnows. Then, you hire an artist to draw a cheerful, smiling minnow to be on every box. Not just any minnow, he's cute and lovable "Mark the Minnow", spokes-fish for Kellogg's Minnow Flakes!

You can hire a guy to wear a life size minnow suit and make personal appearances at grocery stores across the country! In fact, I'd love to do it myself. I've got experience. I once played a rainbow trout in a church play. Let me know what you think.

Yours truly,

Atwood O'Doole

Atwood O'Doole

February 5, 1992

Mr. Atwood O'Doole
6857 Bothwell Rd.
Reseda, CA 91335

Dear Mr. O'Doole:

Thank you for contacting Kellogg Company with your suggestion. We appreciate your interest and the time you took to write.

While we value your interest in our Company, we regret we cannot review or give consideration to your idea. Kellogg Company policy does not allow the Company to consider ideas or suggestions for new products, advertising themes, slogans, promotions, or recipes except those developed internally or by parties under contract with the Company. We do not encourage the submission of ideas by persons who are not directly associated with the Company.

Mr. O'Doole, we want you to know that Kellogg Company is devoting a great deal of time and effort to develop new and improved products, packaging concepts, promotions and merchandising ideas to make our products the best on the market.

Again, thank you for contacting us; we appreciate your interest in our company and products.

Sincerely,

Debbie D. Gestring
Consumer Affairs Department

DDG/cmj

Atwood O'Doole
6857 Bothwell Road
Reseda, California 91335

━━━━━━━━━━━━━━━━━━━━━━━━━━━━━━━━━━

January 25, 1992

Katie Couric
c/o "THE TODAY SHOW", NBC
30 Rockefeller Plaza
New York, New York 10112

Dear Katie:

My name is Atwood O'Doole. In addition to owning an awning and canopy company (O'Doole's Awning & Canopy) I am also an early morning television viewer. You probably already know this but I'm going to tell you anyway -- the Today Show is by far the best network news/magazine broadcast currently offered to the American public. And why shouldn't it be? You've had plenty of time to get it right. Happy 40th Anniversary!

You are an excellent interviewer and you always seem like you're having a good time. Besides having to get up so early and having to work with Bryant, I bet this is probably the best job you've ever had. I especially enjoy the spontaneous banter you engage in when the whole Today Show cast are sitting on the couch just before you go to a commercial at around 7:57am (PST).

If you ever want to do a story on the plight of awning and canopy salesmen in the midst of a recession, you can talk to me. You could follow me around and get a close up of my face when I open up all the bills. I might even cry on camera. Times are really tough. You should be happy that you are working.

If you send me a picture of yourself I'll hang it in my office and tell everyone I'll give them a 10% discount on aluminum awnings if they watch the Today Show.

Yours truly,

Atwood O'Doole

Atwood O'Doole

POLLY O'DOOLE
6857 BOTHWELL ROAD
RESEDA, CA 91335

January 28, 1992

Mr. Fred DeCordova, Producer
The Tonight Show
c/o NBC
3000 West Alameda Avenue
Burbank, CA 91523

Dear Mr. DeCordova:

I know that sometime in May Johnny Carson will host The Tonight
Show for the final time before passing the torch along to Jay
Leno. Actually, passing a fake torch might not be a bad idea for
a skit that night -- being that it is an Olympic year and all!

I'm enclosing a song that Johnny could sing to the audience the
night of his last show. It's sung to the tune of "Tonight" from
West Side Story. He could kind of work it in right after the
monologue. Let's face it, the audience is going to be very
emotional and all with it being the last show. This could keep
the mood light.

I only wrote six verses and two choruses but I'm quick and can
write a few more if you want them. You'll note I even included
a verse about you (but don't let that sway your decision). I'm
donating my song to you free as a bon voyage gift to The Tonight
Show, but I wouldn't turn down a pair of tickets for my husband
and I to attend the final taping of the hottest show in town.
Please let me know if you want to use my song cause we'll
probably have to sign some paperwork.

Sincerely,

Polly O'Doole
Polly O'Doole

"TONIGHT"
(Sung to the tune of "Tonight" from "West Side Story")

Tonight, Tonight
Won't Be Just Any Night
Tonight's my Last Night Hosting this Show

Tomorrow, Tomorrow
Don't let your heart feel sorrow
Cause you'll have a new host - Jay Leno!

    Don't fret, dear Ed, we know where you'll go
    You'll keep on selling Alpo!
    Or take a long vacation

After Tonight
Our lights will still burn bright
Thanks to reruns in syndication!

****

Tonight, God knows
We'll make fun of Doc's clothes
His flashy duds made him a clothes horse

We'll mock, you'll see
Ex-wives one, two and three
And throw in some last jokes 'bout divorce

    Tonight, we'll say farewell to Freddie
    Whose presence has been steady
    A leader not a braggart

Goodbye, dear fans
Remember if you can
Better Leno than Jimmy Swaggart!

CARSON
TONIGHT

TONIGHT SHOW
3000 West Alameda Avenue • Burbank, CA 91523 •

FRED de CORDOVA
Executive Producer

February 4, 1992

Polly O'Doole
6857 Bothwell Road
Reseda, California
91335

Dear Polly O'Doole,

Mr. de Cordova has asked me to thank you for your nice letter and the lyrics, which we'll pass along to Mr. Carson when he returns to work this week.

The format for the final show is "in the works", but I am told that Mr. Carson does not plan to do any singing that evening, although I know your efforts and interest are appreciated.

There will be no ticket distribution for the final show--it will be a "family" evening of invited guests. But tickets for all shows taping between now and May 22nd, excluding that date, are available by writing to the NBC Ticket Division. If you have a problem obtaining tickets for the date you select, please telephone me at the above direct line, and we'll try to be of assistance.

Thank you again for writing, and we all send best wishes.

Sincerely,

B. Freebairn-Smith
Assistant to Mr. de Cordova

/bjf

Atwood O'Doole
6857 Bothwell Road
Reseda, California 91335

━━━━━━━━━━━━━━━━━━━━━━━━━━━━━━━━━━━

February 28, 1992

K-MART
National Headquarters
Customer Care Network
Attn: Robert Clark, Manager
3100 West Big Beaver Road
Troy, Michigan 48084

Dear Mr. Clark:

      My name is Atwood O'Doole. In addition to owning an awning
and canopy company (O'Doole's Awning and Canopy) I am also a proud
father of three. My oldest, A.J., will turn sixteen on May 24. I
am currently considering a number of gifts to honor this special
milestone in his life. First on my list is the Popeil Pocket
Fisherman. Many years ago while living in Kansas, I purchased a
Pocket Fisherman for myself. I never went anywhere without it! It
was in my overalls at work, in my suit pocket at church, in my
bowling trousers on Saturday night and on my bedside table at
night. I didn't know when the urge to go to Wilson Lake was going
to strike me. With the Pocket Fisherman, I was prepared at all
times.

      I had hoped to pass on my Pocket Fisherman to A.J. but I seem
to have misplaced it. So, I would like to purchase a new one for
him. I haven't seen it advertised for a long time. Is it still
available in any of your fine department stores? If so, which
ones? And, can I have it giftwrapped and/or monogrammed?

      Also, I'm looking for an adult sized minnow costume. Do you
have anything available?

                          Yours truly,

                          Atwood O'Doole
                          Atwood O'Doole

Kmart Corporation
International Headquarters
3100 West Big Beaver Road
Troy MI 48084-3163

September 16, 1992

Atwood O'Doole
6857 Bothwell Road
Reseda, CA 91335

Dear Mr. O'Doole,

In regards to your letter we received on August 28, 1992 we are
sorry to inform you that we believe that the Popeil Pocket
Fisherman is no longer in production.

There is a possibility that there is something similar to the
product that you are looking for. If you contact Steve Krenzien
he may have the information that you need.

> STEVE KRENZIEN
> 5395 N. Milwaukee, Ave.
> Chicago, IL   60630

If we can be of any further assistance, please let us know.
Thank you for shopping at Kmart.

Sincerely,

B.A. Brown
Buyer
Sporting Goods

BAB/rls
114

POLLY O'DOOLE
6857 BOTHWELL ROAD
RESEDA, CA 91335

March 4, 1992

San Francisco Zoo
#1 Zoo Road
San Francisco, CA 94132
Attn: <u>David Anderson</u>
      <u>Zoo Director</u>

Dear Mr. Anderson:

Please correct me if I am wrong -- but it has come to my
attention that the San Francisco Zoo is going to have an "adults
only" section of the zoo where you get to watch the animals mate.
Did I hear this story correctly? Isn't there something porno-
graphic about this setup? Besides, how can you control how often
the animals will mate? What if someone buys a ticket and there's
nothing to watch? Some species only mate twice a year when the
female is in heat. (I tried to convince my husband, Atwood, that
that particular law of nature applied to humans too! - Only
kidding!)

Someone suggested that maybe you will tape the animals while
mating for later viewing. Why? Who would want to watch? Is
there really a market for this sort of thing? Does it pay well?
Because we have a really large Saint Bernard, Earl, you might be
interested in taping.

Please set the story straight because I don't want to go to the
San Francisco Zoo with our children and have them shocked by
something they're not ready to see.

Thank you.

Sincerely,

Polly O'Doole

Polly O'Doole

SAN FRANCISCO
ZOOLOGICAL
GARDENS

26 June 1992

A DIVISION OF THE
SAN FRANCISCO
RECREATION &
PARK DEPARTMENT

Ms. Polly O'Doole
6857 Bothwell road
Reseda, CA 91335

1 ZOO ROAD
SAN FRANCISCO
CALIFORNIA
94132-1098

Dear Ms. O'Doole:

Many thanks for your letter of 4 March 1992.

No, we are not planning on an "adults only" section of the zoo where people get to watch the animals mate, nor do we plan to film the animals at such times for later viewing. Our emphasis is on education, not titillation, and as you will see from the enclosed flyer, we organize a "Sex Tour" to take place on or near St. Valentine's Day each year. This is probably the event to which you allude.

Controlled breeding of endangered species, indeed of all species, is of great importance to us here at the zoo, and to people in general. The more people know the more they will support us in our efforts to incorporate a heavy dose of responsibility into our breeding programs.

Please feel free to bring your children to the zoo. Then next February come and enjoy the Third Annual Valentine's Sex Tour. You will find it to be informative and lots of fun. Your husband Atwood will probably enjoy it too. But please leave Earl at home.

Sincerely,

David E. Anderson
Director

DEA:wap

ZOO NEWS

THE SAN FRANCISCO ZOOLOGICAL SOCIETY
1 Zoo Road, San Francisco, California 94132-1098

FOR IMMEDIATE RELEASE:
January 28, 1992

FOR ADULTS ONLY!

SF ZOO SECOND ANNUAL VALENTINE'S SEX TOUR

Back by popular demand -- The San Francisco Zoological Gardens will host the second annual Valentine's Weekend Sex Tour Saturday and Sunday, February 15 and 16, at 9 a.m.

Join Tour Guide and Animal Keeper Jane Tollini as she discusses everything you ever wanted to know about the birds, the bees and the bears at the San Francisco Zoo. "This tongue-in-cheek tour will combine accurate information with a touch of humor and will be for adult audiences only," says Tollini. "The one-hour train tour will discuss revealing information about the sexual methods, strategies, and awesome appendages of the wild kingdom!"

New this year, visitors will learn about contraception methods and devices used at the Zoo. "Sometimes not breeding an animal is the most responsible action a zoo can take," reports Tollini. "Prolific animals like hippopotami are difficult to place at other zoos. With a lifespan of 45 years and a reproductive span of more than 20 years, hippos can easily overpopulate existing zoo facilities. Hippo prophylactics may never be practical, but the future of animal contraception is state-of-the art."

The Valentine's Weekend Sex Tour is limited to guests 18 years or older and is limited to 70 people per tour. Admission is $10 for members, $15 for non-members and funds support San Francisco Zoo Keeper wildlife programs. For more information about Zoo membership or to sign up for the sexiest tour in town, call the San Francisco Zoo.

# # #

Prepared and distributed as a service of the San Francisco Zoological Society

POLLY O'DOOLE
6857 BOTHWELL ROAD
RESEDA, CA 91335

March 6, 1992

Mr. Paul Tsongas
Tsongas Committee
2 Oliver Street
Fifth Floor
Boston, MA 02109

Dear Mr. Tsongas:

I've wanted to send you a campaign contribution for some time now, but raising three children in today's economy made it almost impossible to scrape up some extra cash. I weeded through my family's old and useless possessions and sold some of them at a garage sale. Enclosed is $5.00 I got from selling my husband's Ronco "Pocket Fisherman".

You may already be aware of this, but your name lends itself to a wealth of catchy campaign slogans. Here's a few to mull over:

> Tsincerely Tsongas!
> Tsee you in 1992!
> Tso long, Georgie!
> Quayle Tseason is over!
> Jerry Brown is Tstuck in the Tsixties!
> A Tsongas in the Hand is worth more than Two Quayles
>   and a Bush!
> Tippicanoe and Tsongas Too!

Feel free to use any of the above and good luck to you on Tsuper Tuesday!

Tsincerely,

Polly O'Doole

Polly O'Doole

The Tsongas Committee
Post Office Box 4504
Boston, MA 02101-4504

BOSTON, MA
PM
2. MAY
'92

USA 19

Polly O'Doole
6857 Bothwell Road
Reseda, CA   91335

DEMOCRAT FOR PRESIDENT
Tsongas

Thank you for your recent contribution. I have been heartened to see how people in America have responded to my message of economic hope, and how strongly they are fighting to keep it in the forefront of this election year.

Your help in erasing the campaign debt and keeping the message alive is deeply appreciated.

Sincerely,

Paul

POLLY O'DOOLE
6857 BOTHWELL ROAD
RESEDA, CA 91335

March 10, 1992

The McCall Pattern Company
11 Penn Plaza
New York, New York 10001
Attn: <u>Meg Carter, Customer Service</u>

Dear Ms. Carter:

First of all, I would like to take this opportunity to thank you
for the many beautiful patterns I have bought from your company
over the years. I have been sewing since I was in the 7th grade
(I hesitate to put that thought into actual years -- then you'll
know how old I am!) when I got my first Singer sewing machine as
a Confirmation present from my parents.

This might sound like an odd request, but I overheard my husband,
Atwood, on the phone trying to find an adult size minnow costume
for a business venture. I would like to surprise him by making
this costume for him. You know, I can sew for my daughters and
myself because there are so many patterns available for feminine
clothes but I feel guilty because I haven't done much sewing for
my husband. Let's face it, there aren't too many men walking
around in suits and pants that their wives made for them. Unless
you count leisure suits from the '70's. Lots of men walked
around with home-made leisure suits but the problem with those is
that they looked home-made.

Please advise me if you have any fish patterns from older issues
of pattern books I may have overlooked. Incidentally, it doesn't
have to be a minnow costume, per se. I could use any type of
fish costume and make it look like a minnow by using a particular
color fabric or adding or subtracting a fin.

Thank you.

Polly O'Doole
Polly O'Doole

McCALL'S®

5564 SIZE MEDIUM (5,6)

TAILLE MOYENNE

PATTERN/PATRON

UNDER THE SEA
BE AN OCTOPUS, A
DOLPHIN, A LOBSTER.
SEA WORTHY COSTUMES
FOR BOYS AND GIRLS

DU FOND DE L'OCÉAN

TRANSFORMEZ-VOUS EN
PIEUVRE, EN DAUPHIN
OU EN HOMARD.
DÉGUISEMENTS POUR
GARÇONS ET FILLETTES.

by andrea schewe

POLLY O'DOOLE
6857 BOTHWELL ROAD
RESEDA, CA 91335

March 13, 1992

Baskin-Robbins
31 Baskin-Robbins Place
Glendale, CA 91209
Attn: <u>Carol Kirby</u>
      <u>Director of Marketing</u>

Dear Ms. Kirby:

It has occurred to me that during this Presidential election, it might be fun for you to name some of your ice cream flavors-of-the-month after the Presidential candidates. Please feel free to use some of the following:

<u>Jerry Brown</u>	Chocolate Jerry Brown-ie
<u>Pat Buchanan</u>	Buch-nana Split Supreme
	Buchanan-brittle
<u>Bill Clinton</u>	Mint 'N' Clinton Chip
	Cookies 'N' Clinton (or Clinton 'N' Cream)
<u>Paul Tsongas</u>	Tsongas Tsherbet Tsorbet
	Tsongas Fudge Tswirl
<u>George Bush</u>	Bushberry Delight
	"Read My Lips" Raspberry
<u>Dan Quayle</u>	"You're No Jack Kennedy" Krunch
<u>Miscellaneous</u>	Presidential Pumpkin
	Lemon LaRouche
	White House Hash
	Rocky Road to the Whitehouse
	Republican Ripple
	G.O.P.eanut Butter Mousse

I do not expect payment if you decide to use any of the above names. I would not, however, be opposed to a gift certificate or coupon that would allow my family to enjoy your fine products.

Sincerely,

Polly O'Doole

Polly O'Doole

Baskin (31) Robbins™

Baskin-Robbins USA, Co.
Corporate Headquarters
31 Baskin-Robbins Place
Glendale. CA 91201

March 24, 1992

Ms. Polly O'Dolle
6857 Bothwell Rd.
Reseda, CA 91335

Dear Ms. O'Dolle:

Thank you very much for your ideas for new Baskin-Robbins flavors.
You might think that with over 650 flavors in our "library," we'd
have enough--but we always enjoy hearing new suggestions.

As you can no doubt imagine, we receive a great number of
suggestions for flavors here at Baskin-Robbins headquarters. Many
of them are very similar--and others have already been created and
evaluated by our own team of flavor chefs and marketers.

Again, thank you for sharing your thoughts with us. Please accept
the enclosed gift certificate with our compliments.

Sincerely,

Kathie Bellamy
Consumer Affairs

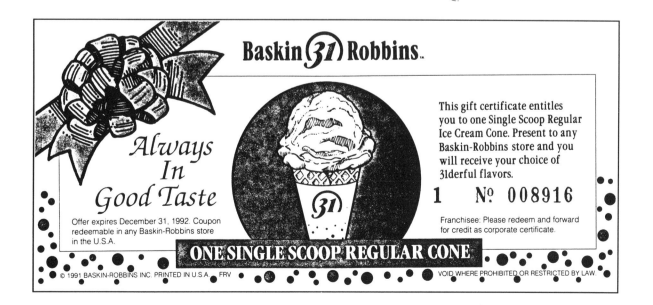

Atwood O'Doole
6857 Bothwell Road
Reseda, California 91335

March 16, 1992

Kimberly-Clark Corporation
Attn: Consumer Services
Dept. KFT-175, P.O. Box 2020
Neenah, WI 54957-2020

Dear Sir/Madame:

My name is Atwood O'Doole. In addition to owning my own awning and canopy company (O'Doole's Awning and Canopy) I also use Kleenex brand facial tissue when necessary.

My wife Polly has been working very hard in the kitchen lately, both at home and at work where she's a junior high school cafeteria manager. Her increased exhaustion has caused her to snore very loudly in bed. Unfortunately, I'm a very light sleeper. Recently, I wadded up several Kleenex tissues and stuffed them into my ears. To my delight, her nasal eruptions were muted and I slept like a baby. I thought I had solved my problem until I overslept the next morning. I couldn't hear my alarm clock!

Since your product seems to be an excellent acoustical device I'd like to continue using it as such. But only if it is safe to do so. This time I want to try stuffing tissue directly into my wife's nostrils. I assume your product is not designed for this use and I don't know what chemicals or compounds are in it. Could prolonged insertion in a nasal passage cause any potential health problems other than general discomfort?

I look forward to your prompt response. Until then, I'm sleeping on the couch.

Very truly yours,

Atwood O'Doole

Atwood O'Doole

May 4, 1992

Mr. Atwood O'Doole
6857 Bothwell Road
Reseda, CA 91335

Dear Mr. O'Doole:

Thank you for contacting us about KLEENEX® facial tissue. We
appreciate the opportunity to respond.

In answer to your question, we would not recommend placing tissue in
your wife's nose. First, blocking her nose could cause difficulty in
breathing. Secondly, snoring occurs when a person is breathing through
their mouth and not the nose. You may want to discuss this with your
physician to find out if there is anything available that would
alleviate this problem.

Thank you again for your interest in our products and for taking the
time to contact us.

Sincerely,

Joyce M. Drace

Joyce M. Drace
Consumer Representative

JMD/cl

I Love You Dearly,
Atwood

You Are The Man I
Chose...

Atwood O'Doole

But I'm Leaving You
If You Stuff One More
Kleenex Up My Nose!

Love,
Polly

6857 Bothwell Rd.
Reseda, CA 91335

March 18, 1992

Eddie Bauer
P.O. Box 3700
Seattle, Washington 98124-3700

Dear Mr. Bauer:

My name is A.J. O'Doole. I'm fifteen years old. My
father owns his own awning and canopy company
(O'Doole's Awning and Canopy). After college he would
like me to work full time for him. But I want a job
that has nothing to do with either awnings or canopies.

I think it would be neat to own my own clothing store.
I understand that you own two hundred of them. How did
you start your business? Do I need a college education
to start my own clothing store? Who makes all those
clothes anyway?

Sincerely,

A.J. O'Doole

A.J. O'Doole

EDDIE BAUER, INC.
15010 N.E. 36th Street
Redmond, Washington 98052

May 15, 1992

Master A. J. O'Doole
6857 Bothwell Road
Reseda, CA   91335

Dear A.J.:

I hope you weren't concerned that we had not received your letter, but because Mr. Eddie Bauer passed away almost ten years ago, I am taking this opportunity of answering your recent letter.

Because of a family crisis, it was in the eighth grade that Eddie Bauer became the sole support of his mother and sister. At age 15, just your age, he worked after school and on weekends in the stockroom of Seattle's largest sporting goods store. For the next five years he gained knowledge of product selection, display, special promotions, marketing and most importantly, how friendly and knowledgeable customer service could build and retain a solid customer base. Experience taught him, at a very early age, that the only reason he had a job was because of the customer.

At age 20, he opened his own store. His personal commitment to providing outstanding quality and service to his customers, made his store successful from the start. Clothing was a natural extension of the sporting goods that he had sold for years because they are such an important part of being able to fully enjoy the outdoor activities he and his customers participated in. He promoted the clothing he sold assuring his customers that he, Eddie Bauer, had personally tested it and therefore backed it with an unconditional guarantee.

In addition to his avid enjoyment of the outdoors, Mr. Bauer had a bountiful supply of natural curiosity and the compulsion to produce things faster, better, and more profitably than others. Because of this compulsion, at age 17, he designed a tennis racket stringing machine on which he could turn out a tournament quality racket in 8 minutes. Stringing tennis rackets gave him enough income to open his own store. A few years later he designed and patented the process to produce tournament grade shuttle-cocks; each identical in weight and flight characteristics to its predecessor. The manufacturing of these shuttle-cocks also got him involved with the feather and down industry which ultimately lead to his design and patent of the first goose-down insulated garment.

You asked, A.J., "Who makes all those clothes, anyway?" When you have an opportunity, go into your nearby clothing store and read the sewn-in labels on the shirts, pants and coats that you see. A word of guidance here -- a Sears or Montgomery Wards store will feature their own brand labels which we call "private" labels. Some manufacturers deal in this "private label" world and at the same time promote garments labeled in their own name. Don't be dismayed by the profusion of trade names and house-named labels. Be assured by the time you own your own clothing store, there will be thousands of suppliers. We still develop and design all of the clothing that we sell, but we use hundreds of suppliers throughout the world to manufacture the clothing for us to our specifications.

I've enclosed a copy of a 1988 newspaper summarizing Eddie's life and enjoyment of the out of doors. I'm sure he would agree that when a young man like yourself shows promise of growing up into an outstanding member of society, he's just the sort that businessmen like to recruit. It's only natural for your father to want the business to stay in the family, especially if you're the only son or the one that has the greatest interest in a business vocation. Maybe stepping back and taking a different look at the family business would put it in a new perspective for you.

Thanks again, A.J., for the letter and we wish you every success in whatever venture you decide to pursue in the future. If you do have any further questions or if I can provide you with any further information, please let me know.

Cordially,

Ken A. Wherry
Sr. Vice President
Operations

POLLY O'DOOLE
6857 BOTHWELL ROAD
RESEDA, CA 91335

March 19, 1992

Petco
9151 Rehco Road
San Diego, CA 92121
Attn: <u>Mary Stroanch</u>

Dear Ms. Stroanch:

While shopping for dog food the other night at PetCo in Glendale, CA, I happened to notice a product of yours called Supreme "mouse and rat food". Since it was right next to the dog food, I couldn't help being confused. Is it dog food made up of mice and rat parts or is it nourishment for mice and rats? I can't say I know anyone who has encouraged unwanted vermin by putting a bowl of rat yummies in their backyard.

Please let me know the intended use of this product. I asked the clerk at Petco if she knew. She just stared at me and didn't answer. I guess she couldn't speak English. If rat and mice parts are an alternative to regular dog food (consisting of chicken or fish parts), I don't want to deprive my dog, Earl, of something new and tasty.

I look forward to hearing from you.

Sincerely,

Polly O'Doole

Polly O'Doole

PET FOOD AND SUPPLIES   9151 REHCO ROAD • SAN DIEGO, CALIFORNIA 92121

March 30, 1992

Ms. Polly O'Doole
6857 Bothwell Rd.
Reseda, CA 91335

Dear Ms. O'Doole:

Thank you for your letter of March 19, 1992. We at Petco
appreciate your concern with regard to the product mentioned.
"Supreme Rat and Mouse Food" is for the diet of rats and mice.
This product is considered a "Small Animal" product, which must
have been next to the dog food the day you were shopping. We
apologize for any misunderstanding this might have caused you.
Again, thank you for your interest in Petco.

Sincerely,

Mary M. Stronach
Merchandising Secretary

/mms

POLLY O'DOOLE
6857 BOTHWELL ROAD
RESEDA, CA 91335

March 20, 1992

The Duchess of York
Buckingham Palace
London, England

Dear Fergie:

I'm so sorry to hear of the demise of your marriage to Prince
Andrew. You seemed so happy. I guess that things are not always
what they appear to be. Here's a poem I wrote to cheer you up.

<u>ODE TO FERGIE</u>

There once was a girl named Fergie
She had red hair and was perky
She married a lad and the marriage went bad
Now her future's unclear and seems murkey

At one point she was overweight
I guess it's cause she overate
Her calories were trimmed and she became slim
Now she'll never lack for a date

She'll be sad and alone for a while
But her frown will turn into a smile
She may remarry some Tom, Dick or Harry
And live a charmed life full of style

There's no need to be in a bad mood
You'll stay thin, be happy and look good
Here's something to think of while seeking a new love
Keep your hands off my husband, Atwood!

Keep a stiff upper lip.

Sincerely,

Polly O'Doole

Polly O'Doole

BUCKINGHAM PALACE

31st March 1992

Dear Mrs O'Doole

The Duchess of York has asked me to write and thank you for your letter.

Her Royal Highness would like to be able to answer all her letters personally, but she has been so overwhelmed by the public's generosity, that I hope you will understand therefore why she is not able to reply.

However, Her Royal Highness has read your letter and appreciates all that you have said. Your kindness and perception has meant so much to her.

The Duchess of York would like me to send you her warmest wishes.

Yours sincerely

Lady in Waiting

6857 Bothwell Rd.
Reseda, CA 91335

March 24, 1992

Carl Karcher
c/o Carl's Jr. Restaurants
1200 N. Harbor Blvd.
P.O. Box 4349
Anaheim, California 92803

Dear Mr. Karcher:

My name is A.J. (Atwood Junior) O'Doole. My father
owns his own awning and canopy company (O'Doole's
Awning & Canopy). He wants me to work for him and
someday take over the business, but I'm looking at
other possibilities. Since you're a Jr. too, you must
really know how hard it is to walk in the shadows of
your father.

Was it your own idea to start selling hamburgers or did
your father suggest you do it? I think it would be
neat to own my own line of restaurants and call it
"Atwood's Jr." If I try to do that do you think I need
to go to college first? How did you get started? I'd
really like to know.

Sincerely,

A.J. O'Doole

A.J. O'Doole

Carl Karcher Enterprises, Inc.
Corporate Headquarters · 1200 North Harbor Boulevard · P.O. Box 4349 · Anaheim, California 92803-4349

Carl N. Karcher
Chairman and
Chief Executive Officer

April 24, 1992

Mr. A. J. O'Doole
6857 Bothwell Road
Reseda CA 91335

Dear Mr. O'Doole:

Thank you very much for your recent letter. You have a lot of
questions about my history, so I have enclosed a copy of my book
Never Stop Dreaming. I hope you will enjoy it.

Good luck with "Atwoods's Jr.".

Sincerely,

Carl N. Karcher

PS-In case you aren't aware of it, we use your father's awnings....!

NEVER STOP DREAMING

50 YEARS OF MAKING IT HAPPEN

The Inspirational Life Story of Carl Karcher, Founder of Carl's Jr.

As told to B. Carolyn Knight

Never
Stop
Dreaming

4/27/92

May God Continue
to Bless A.J. O'Doole
in all his 'Dreams'

Sincerely,
Carl N. Karcher

Atwood O'Doole
6857 Bothwell Road
Reseda, California 91335

===

March 25, 1992

American Dental Association
Attn: Dr. Geraldine Morrow
211 East Chicago Avenue
Chicago, Illinois 60611

Dear Dr. Morrow:

    My name is Atwood O'Doole. In addition to owning my own
awning and canopy company (O'Doole's Awning and Canopy) I also
floss my teeth every day.

    I go fishing quite often on weekends and holidays. While in
my boat or on a pier, I like to take only the bare essentials --
bait, tackle, sunscreen, twinkies and Dr. Pepper. My efforts to
streamline the accessories on my angling excursions has caused me
to be quite resourceful. For example, I floss my teeth with
fishing line. I usually use a Stren Super Tough 20 lb. test, but
I sometimes find that a Berkley Trilene XL works better,
especially if I had chicken the night before.

    My wife Polly thinks I should stop this. She's afraid I'm
going to get some kind of weird gum disease. She wants me to
start packing real dental floss, but I want to remain as portable
as possible. Before I do anything, I promised her I'd find out
the truth. Are there any potential health problems associated
with flossing with fishing line?

                            Very truly yours,

                            Atwood O'Doole

                            Atwood O'Doole

American
Dental
Association

Geraldine T. Morrow, D.M.D.
President
211 East Chicago Avenue
Chicago, Illinois 60611-2678

April 21, 1992

Atwood O'Doole
6857 Bothwell Rd.
Reseda, CA 91335

Dear Mr. O'Doole:

I received your letter regarding your fishing and flossing excursions. I can appreciate your efforts at trying to streamline the accessories on your angling trips. Catching dental plaque with a fishing line, however, may not be the best practice for your oral health.

It is unlikely that there are any studies examining the risk of acquiring diseases from fishing line or of its effectiveness as dental floss. Fishing line is pretty tough, though. It could injure your gums and could also introduce bacteria. To be on the safe side, I would recommend sticking with conventional dental floss.

To be sure of purchasing products that are safe and effective, choose those products with the ADA Seal. Enclosed, for your information, is a brochure about dental products and the Seal.

Happy fishing!

Sincerely,

Geraldine T. Morrow, D.M.D.
President

Enclosure

GTM:pc

POLLY O'DOOLE
6857 BOTHWELL ROAD
RESEDA, CA 91335

March 27, 1992

Mr. William Clinton
Clinton For President Committee
P.O. Box 615
Little Rock, Arkansas 72203

Dear Mr. Clinton:

Congratulations! One candidate down and one to go! I think
you're doing a fine job with your campaign but I believe you need
to make one change. Think about this. People may not have liked
Tsongas enough for him to stay in the race, but they sure
remembered his name. Especially because they had Tso much
trouble Tsaying or Tspelling it! Now that he's out of the
picture, you might want to try some spelling tricks yourself.

There's not too much you can do with a straightforward name
like Clinton but here are a few suggestions. Perhaps you could
hyphenate it ("Clin-ton") or put a tilda (~) over the first "n"
("Cliñton"). This could help capture the Hispanic vote! Or you
could put an accent aigu ("ó") over the "ó" ("Clintón") to appeal
to French nationals. Or perhaps you'd be partial to an umlaut
("ö") ("Clintön"). I'm not sure which one works best, but please
feel free to use any of these suggestions. Hurry up because you
don't have much time left.

Tsin-Tserely yours, (Tsee how he could have used his name for
                     Tslogans?)

Polly O'Doole
Polly O'Doole

FOR PRESIDENT COMMITTEE

April 22, 1992

Polly O'Doole
6857 Bothwell Road
Reseda, CA 91335

Dear Polly:

Just a brief note to let you know how much I appreciate your letter. I enjoyed your suggestions.

Thank you for interest in my campaign.

Sincerely,

Bill Clinton

Bill Clinton

BC:sc

National Campaign Headquarters • P.O. Box 615 • Little Rock, Arkansas 72203

12

6857 Bothwell Rd.
Reseda, CA 91335

March 29, 1992

Colonel Sanders
c/o KFC Corporate Headquarters
1441 Gardiner Lane
Louisville, Kentucky 40213

Dear Colonel:

My name is A.J. O'Doole. I'll be a senior next year so
I'm trying to figure out what I want to do after high
school. My father wants me to work at his awning and
canopy company (O'Doole's Awning & Canopy) but I think
that would be boring.

Did you discover your secret recipe while in the
service? I think it would be neat to own a
multimillion dollar global fast food franchise, whether
my recipe was secret or not. What did you do to get
yours started? You didn't have to work with awnings or
canopies did you? I'd really like to know.

Sincerely,

A.J. O'Doole

A.J. O'Doole

6857 Bothwell Rd.
Reseda, CA 91335

March 29, 1992

Colonel Sanders
c/o KFC Corporate Headquarters
1441 Gardiner Lane
Louisville, Kentucky 40213

Dear Colonel:

My name is A.J. O'Doole. I'll be a senior next year so
I'm trying to figure out what I want to do after high
school. My father wants me to work at his awning and
canopy company (O'Doole's Awning & Canopy) but I think
that would be boring.

Did you discover your secret recipe while in the
service? I think it would be neat to own a
multimillion dollar global fast food franchise, whether
my recipe was secret or not. What did you do to get
yours started? You didn't have to work with awnings or
canopies did you? I'd really like to know.

Sincerely,

A.J. O'Doole

A.J. O'Doole

5/20/92

Mr. O'Doole: Colonel Sanders passed
away in December, 1980 at age 90.
He had many jobs before hitting on
major success at age 65 with Kentucky
Fried Chicken. I'm enclosing some
information about this legendary pioneer
in our industry. The Colonel would have
commended you on the thought you're
giving to your career, but he never under-
stood the word "boring". Business challenges
are exciting. The Colonel would look at O'Doole's
Awning & Canopy & think "global franchise?"!
Best wishes - S. Schneider

Saga of the "Chicken" Colonel

In 1956, Harland Sanders was an out-of-work 66-year-old. Today he is a millionaire, and the business he started—known round the world as "Kentucky Fried Chicken"—grosses over one billion dollars a year

Condensed from
LOUISVILLE MAGAZINE
JAMES STEWART-GORDON

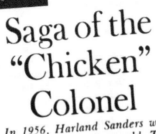

COL. Harland Sanders, of Louisville, Ky., the founding father, tireless promoter and international image of Kentucky Fried Chicken, is probably the best-known bewhiskered American since Abraham Lincoln. Aided by a $50-million-a-year advertising and publicity budget, the Colonel is as visible as the Statue of Liberty on a clear day. His goateed face beams out from highway billboards, the fronts of his stores, on television commercials, comedy hours, movies and talk shows, and on the more than two million containers of Kentucky Fried Chicken sold every day. Summer or winter he sports a white suit, a string tie anchored by a diamon

LOUISVILLE MAGAZINE [JANUARY '75]. © 1974
BY THE LOUISVILLE AREA CHAMBER OF COMMERCE, INC.,
300 WEST LIBERTY, LOUISVILLE, KY. 40202

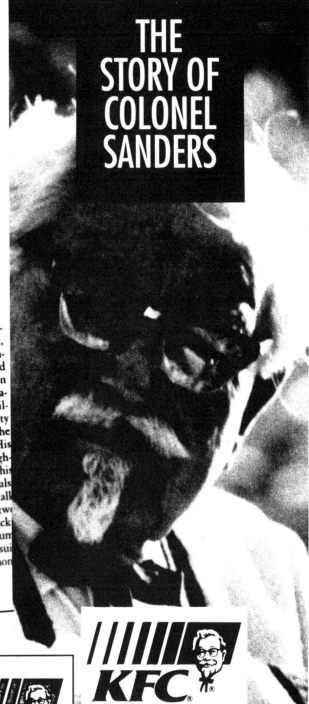

THE STORY OF COLONEL SANDERS

KFC®

KFC®

Shirley Topmiller
Group Manager
Consumer Affairs
& Corporate Contributions

P.O. Box 32070
Louisville KY 40232-2070

My Diary   APRIL 2, 1992

Last night I had a nightmare. I dreamed that my father showed up at my school dressed as a fish. Even though his head was covered by the costume, I knew it was him because he kept shouting "maureen, swim to Daddy." I tried running away from him, but as I ran I started shedding fish scales. all the kids from school just looked on in horror. I woke up and wrote this poem.   MO

Fish Flakes
by Mo O'Poole

Minnow, Minnow, Minnow
What's in a name?
Don your costume, fish lover
But remember... you are what you eat
And as you feast on your cornflakes
Beware that you are becoming both.

POLLY O'DOOLE
6857 BOTHWELL ROAD
RESEDA, CA 91335

April 10, 1992

Ms. Loretta Swit
c/o Jack Rosenfeld, President
Hanover House
340 Poplar Street, Bldg. 20
Hanover, PA 17333-0003

Dear Ms. Swit:

In theory, I like the idea of a lipstick that lasts for 24 hours.
But before I fork over $29.95 for "Lasting Kiss," I want some
assurances that the unfortunate experience I had while wearing a
competitor's version of your product will not reoccur.

The other day at work, a friend gave me a tube of colorless
lipstick. She told me the color changes on each person because
everyone's body chemistry is different. This sounded like a very
90's product to me and I eagerly applied a generous amount to my
lips. When I looked in the mirror I was pleased to see a very
natural pink shade. My friend informed me that the color would
deepen a little. What she didn't tell me is that it would
eventually "glow in the dark" and wouldn't wash off for 24 hours!

On my way home, I stopped off to buy some pet food. When I
opened the door to Petco, a brazen twelve year old boy puckered
up his lips and started making kissing noises at me. I was
confused because I did nothing to encourage this disrespectful
behavior. Again, while at the checkout counter, I encountered
odd behavior from the cashier. Although I asked her several
questions, she just stared at me. I just figured she didn't
speak English. Once I arrived home and turned on the bathroom
light, I almost passed out. To say my lips were bright is an
understatement. I needed sunglasses just to brush my teeth!
Lucky for me, my husband just bought about a year's supply of
Kleenex tissues. I spent the next two hours depleting his
stockpile trying to wipe this lipstick off my face.

From one "Hot Lips" to another, can I trust "Lasting Kiss"? That
other lipstick caused me a lot of embarrassment and I will avoid
it like the plague. As a matter of fact, I'm getting rid of it
to make sure I don't ever use it again by mistake.

Sincerely,

Polly O'Doole

Polly O'Doole

December 8, 1992

Polly O'Doole
6857 Bothwell Road
Reseda, CA 91335

Dear Ms. O'Doole:

Thank you for your recent letter.

Enclosed you will find a copy of the literature which accompanies the purchase of the "Lasting Kiss" lipstick. Hopefully, this information will help you decide on your purchase.

Thank you again for your letter and we look forward to serving you again in the near future.

Sincerely,

Stephanie Crawford
Consumer Affairs
Office of the President

Hanover House

**POLLY O'DOOLE
6857 BOTHWELL ROAD
RESEDA, CA 91335**

April 14, 1992

Mrs. Hillary Clinton
Clinton For President Committee
P.O. Box 615
Little Rock, Arkansas 72203

Dear Mrs. Clinton:

Congratulations on "Standing By Your Man" during this 1992
Presidential Campaign. This whirlwind pace and frantic travel
schedule must really be taking a toll on all the candidates'
health and emotions. Not to mention that it doesn't leave a lot
of time for pampering yourself with beauty treatments and makeup.
So I've taken the liberty of sending you something to make your
life a little easier during this hectic period of your life.

Enclosed is a tube of Pure Aloe Vera Lipstick. It is colorless
in the tube but adjusts to your very own special color. Once you
apply it, you don't have to worry about your lipstick wearing off
for the rest of the day. Wear it in good health!

Sincerely,

Polly O'Doole
Polly O'Doole

July 25, 1992

Polly O'Doole
6857 Bothwell RD
Reseda, CA 91335

Dear Polly:

Thank you for your thoughtful letter. I want you to know how
much I personally appreciate your support of Bill's candidacy.

Thank you also for kindly sending me the lovely lipstick. It
is so nice to get such tokens of appreciation and to know that
Bill and I are in people's thoughts.

Your words of encouragement gave me a lift. I wish you
success and once again, thank you for your thoughtfulness and
continued support.

Sincerely yours,

Hillary Rodham Clinton

National Campaign Headquarters • P.O. Box 615 • Little Rock, Arkansas 72203

Paid for by the Clinton for President Committee
Contributions to the Clinton for President Committee are not tax deductible.

Printed on Recycled Paper

Atwood O'Doole
6857 Bothwell Road
Reseda, California 91335

═══

May 3, 1992

Governor Sam Stephens
State Capital - Governor's Office
Helena, Montana 59620

Dear Governor Stephens:

My name is Atwood O'Doole. In addition to owning an awning
and canopy company (O'Doole's Awning & Canopy) I also subscribe
to the Los Angeles Times. A February 26, 1992 article entitled
"Lean Times Spark Rural Battles for Edible Game Killed On Roads"
has deeply touched my wife Polly and myself.

Fourteen years ago I had a semi-successful awning and canopy
company (O'Doole's Awning & Canopy of Gorham) in Gorham, Kansas.
With my infant son and pregnant wife, I moved to southern
California to pursue a lifelong dream of expanding into shades
and blinds. Though we have left small town life for the big
city, our hearts are still with rural Americans everywhere. Our
compassion is heightened when we hear of the plight of the
recession weary Montanans who are combing their thoroughfares for
their next meal.

When times were tough in Gorham, we too found ourselves
competing for fresh game killed on the busy highway in front of
our trailer. Why, I don't know how we could have survived
without an occasional squirrel or rabbit to feast on during the
winter months. It is most unfortunate that in your state this
precious food resource is being spoiled by a few greedy thieves.

I still haven't gotten into shades and blinds, but I'm doing
well enough to pass along a couple of dollars in hopes that there
is some sort of fund to enforce the apprehension of roadkill
poachers. If not, use it to buy a poor family a hamburger.

Let me know if I can do anything else.

Very truly yours,

Atwood O'Doole

Atwood O'Doole

State of Montana
Office of the Governor
Helena, Montana 59620

May 27, 1992

STAN STEPHENS
GOVERNOR

Atwood O'Doole
6857 Bothwell Road
Reseda, California   91335

Dear Mr. O'Doole:

Thank you very much for your interesting letter and your "substantial contribution" to the assistance of our Fish, Wildlife and Parks enforcement people.

I appreciate your sense of humor and your willingness to put your money where your mouth is.

Naturally, we encourage you to visit our beautiful state, avoiding of course the wildlife that you may see along the roadways.

Sincerely,

STAN STEPHENS
Governor

cc: K. L. Cool

Montana Department of Fish, Wildlife & Parks

1420 East Sixth Avenue
Helena, MT 59620
June 11, 1992

Atwood O'Doole
6857 Bothwell Road
Reseda, CA 91335

Dear Mr. O'Doole:

I've shared your letter as well as our governor's with the Fish, Wildlife and Parks Crimestoppers Board members. You both brought humor to our board meeting.

The two dollars was deposited in our reward fund. The board recently rewarded ten deserving individuals who helped our wardens solve serious violations of Montana game laws.

I hope you will visit our state.

Sincerely,

Elmer E. Davis
Program Manager
Law Enforcement Division

EED/rh

Atwood O'Doole
6857 Bothwell Road
Reseda, California 91335

===

May 5, 1992

American Dental Association
Attn: Dr. Geraldine Morrow
211 East Chicago Avenue
Chicago, Illinois 60611

Dear Dr. Morrow:

Thanks for your recent response to my dental floss inquiry.
From now on I plan on going that extra mile and packing ADA
approved floss on all my fishing excursions.

I would now like some information regarding another issue.
My wife Polly snores very loudly and I'm trying to find a way to
suppress her nocturnal rumblings so I can sleep soundly. A Ms.
Joyce Drace of the Kimberly Clarke Corporation has informed me
that inserting Kleenex into her nose would not suppress the noise
because it is actually coming from her mouth. Since mouths are
your business, I thought you might be able to give me some
guidance. Is there something I could insert into my wife's mouth
to muffle the snoring? Would an apple do the trick? What about
a sock?

I anxiously await your reply.

Very truly yours,

Atwood O'Doole

Atwood O'Doole

American
Dental
Association

211 East Chicago Avenue
Chicago, Illinois 60611-2678

June 2, 1992

Atwood O'Doole
6857 Bothwell Road
Reseda, California   91335

Dear Mr. Atwood:

Your letter addressed to Dr. Geraldine Morrow has been referred
to me for response.

Sleeping disorders do not relate directly to dental care. Your
wife may wish to contact the Sleep Disorder Clinic of UCLA.

I hope this information is helpful.

Sincerely,

Suzanne Richter
Manager, Health Promotions
Division of Communications

6857 Bothwell Rd.
Reseda, CA 91335

May 7, 1992

Peter Dekom
Bloom, Dekom & Hergott
150 South Rodeo Drive
3rd Floor
Beverly Hills, CA 90212

Dear Mr. Dekom:

My name is A.J. O'Doole. I'm fifteen years old and I'm
trying to decide what I want to do when I get out of
high school. Do you like being an attorney? How much
money do you make? Did you have to go to college? I
think it would be neat to wear a suit every day and
carry a briefcase and have nice things.

My father keeps telling me I'm going to work for his
awning and canopy company (O'Doole's Awning and Canopy)
but I don't want to. Could I sue him if he forces me
to work for him? If so, would you be my lawyer? How
much would you charge me?

Sincerely,

A.J. O'Doole

A.J. O'Doole

BLOOM, DEKOM AND HERGOTT
ATTORNEYS AT LAW

150 SOUTH RODEO DRIVE, THIRD FLOOR
BEVERLY HILLS, CALIFORNIA 90212

JACOB A. BLOOM
PETER J. DEKOM
ALAN S. HERGOTT
LAWRENCE H. GREAVES
CANDICE S. HANSON
MATTHEW G. KRANE
MELANIE COOK
TINA J. KAHN
JULIE M. PHILIPS
THOMAS F. HUNTER
JOHN D. DIEMER
STEPHEN D. BARNES
GARY L. GILBERT
STUART M. ROSENTHAL

STEPHEN F. BREIMER
STEVEN L. BROOKMAN
DEBORAH L. KLEIN
LARY SIMPSON
JOHN LAVIOLETTE
JONATHAN BLAUFARB
ROBYN L. ROTH

LEIGH BRECHEEN
OF COUNSEL

THOMAS P. POLLOCK
FOUNDING PARTNER
THROUGH 1986

May 29, 1992

A.J. O'Doole
6857 Bothwell Rd.
Reseda, CA 91335

Dear A.J.:

In answer to your questions in your letter of May 7th:

1.   Yes, I like being an attorney. But what do you like? What gets you excited, what kinds of things are you intrigued by? You have to lead yourself along the path to self-discovery by following your own clues.

2.   A lot. But money isn't everything.

3.   Of course. I can't believe a 15 year old high school student wouldn't know that college (and lots of it) is necessary to become a lawyer. Ever hear of a "Bar Exam?"

4.   The Bill of Rights gives you the freedom to choose your own destiny, so your father cannot force you to work for him, but he might try if you are still living under his roof and don't take responsibility for your own life.

You can do anything you want with your life as long as you believe in yourself and move through life with integrity. And make sure that what you are doing brings you great joy. Then, you can't lose.

Hey, are you for real?

Very truly yours,

PETER J. DEKOM
of BLOOM, DEKOM and HERGOTT

PJD/bfb

Atwood O'Doole
6857 Bothwell Road
Reseda, California 91335

━━━━━━━━━━━━━━━━━━━━━━━━━━━━━━━━━━━━━━━

May 11, 1992

Mr. Jules Melillo
Wardrobe Department
Warner Bros. Pictures
4000 Warner Blvd.
Burbank, California 91522-0001

Dear Mr. Melillo:

My name is Atwood O'Doole. In addition to owning an awning
and canopy company (O'Doole's Awning & Canopy) I am also a proud
father of three. My oldest, A.J., will celebrate his 16th
birthday on May 24. He's a very ambitious young man and he's
looking forward to working for me when he graduates from high
school next year.

I'd like to help recognize this milestone in A.J.'s life in
a very special way. His favorite movie of all time is BATMAN and
he's terribly excited about the release of BATMAN II next month.
It would absolutely thrill him if he had his very own Batman cape
to wear on his birthday. You must have lots of them lying around
somewhere. Could I buy one? Or maybe you'd let me rent it until
you start BATMAN III. If this is a problem, maybe we can work
something out with Superman's cape.

I anxiously await your reply.

Yours truly,

Atwood O'Doole

Atwood O'Doole

May 19, 1992

Mr. Atwood O'Doole
6857 Bothwell Road
Reseda CA, 91335

Dear Mr. O'Doole

   Thank you for your interest-in Batman and Batman Returns.
Unfortunately it is not company policy to sell or lend costumes
used in features or television.

   Sorry I couldn't be of more assistance.

Julie Davis
Wardrobe Dept.

POLLY O'DOOLE
6857 BOTHWELL ROAD
RESEDA, CA 91335

May 22, 1992

Mr. Michael Rollins, President
Nashville Chamber of Commerce
161 Fourth Avenue North
Nashville, Tennessee 37219

Dear Mr. Rollins:

I am planning a trip to the Nashville area in the near future
and, like many others who have visited your fair city, I, too,
have dreams of becoming a country western superstar. Actually,
at this point I'd be happy selling some lyrics for a commercial
to help pay for the evergrowing expense of trying to raise a
family of five in today's economy. I bet I could write a pretty
good song about that!

Attached is a list of some of my songs which are all original.
And just in case you're wondering, I'm no "Polly Vanolli" - I
sing all my songs in my own voice. I have never lipsynched
anything in my life except for the time my husband Atwood won a
"Learn to Bellydance for Your Husband" album where you had to
sing along in Turkish. I never played the album enough to
memorize the melody and lyrics because we always got into an
argument about where that album really came from. He didn't win
it - he bought it. He should have picked up the LP "Learn to
Appreciate Your Wife" or "I Just Worked a Double Shift, Fed and
Bathed the Kids and You Think I Feel Like Dancin'?" This is good
-- anger produces some of the best country western music.

I would appreciate it if you could let me know who some of the
best agents are in the country western music business. I will
only be able to stay in Nashville a short while so if there's
anyone else I should meet with, please let me know.

Thank you.

Polly O'Doole
Polly O'Doole

SONGS BY POLLY O'DOOLE

1. 1 - 2 - 3 Let's Go Spend My Al-i-mo-ny!

2. You're the Captain of my Love Boat (So Let's Drop Anchor
    Here Tonight)!

3. I Hope You Like Eating Alpo Cause You're In The Dog House
    Now!

4. You've Got Egg on Your Face So Let's Scramble Up Some Love

5. When You Take The Garbage Out Tonight You Should Feel Right
    At Home!

6. Instead of Counting Sheep, I Always Count Your Lies

7. My Checks Are Bouncin' At The Bank of Love

8. You Bit The Bait And Now I'm Reelin' In Romance

9. I Can't Pay the Landlord With My Tears

10. I Hope Love Will Prevail (Cause I Can't Make Your Bail)!

11. Your Daddy Is a Good Man, But He's Really Not You're Dad!

MUSIC CITY
USA

Ranked Second Among
American Cities for
Pro-Business Attitude,
Race Relations

A Publication of the Nashville Area Chamber of Commerce

Printed on Recycled Paper

Information Services
161 Fourth Avenue North
Nashville, TN 37219

MUSIC CITY
USA

NASHVILLE CHAMBER

L. BHD
POLLY O DOODE
c857 ROTHWELL RD
RESEDA CA 91335

Atwood O'Doole
6857 Bothwell Road
Reseda, California 91335

May 28, 1992

Mr. Curt Smitch
Director, Washington Department
of Wildlife
600 Capitol Way N.
Olympia, WA 98501-1091

Dear Mr. Smitch:

My name is Atwood O'Doole. In addition to owning an awning and canopy company (O'Doole's Awning & Canopy) I am also a proud father of three. My oldest, A.J., just celebrated his 16th birthday. My original plans of obtaining a special gift from a certain motion picture studio fell through, so I bought him a brand new rod and reel instead. And I promised him I'd take him on a fishing trip to Washington next month so he could use it.

We'll be angling at several lakes and streams across your great state on or around June 21st, which is Father's Day. I purposely scheduled the trip during this time so A.J. and I could bond in a special father/son kind of way. Some of my fondest childhood memories are when my own father took me fishing and I would hate to deprive young A.J. of the same joy I experienced.

While studying the 1992-93 Washington Department of Wildlife Game Fish Regulations, I noticed that on page seven you state that it is unlawful to "conduct a fishing contest without a permit from the Director of the Department of Wildlife." Well, there is a traditional O'Doole family fishing contest which began with my great great grandfather Randall O'Doole in which father and son wager on the days total catch. A.J. and I plan on using my favorite outdoor sportsman snack -- Twinkies. At the end of each day the man who has accumulated the most fish receives an entire box from his competitor. I have no intention of breaking this tradition but I also don't want to break the law. Do I have to have a permit? Please let me know as soon as possible.

Very truly yours,

Atwood O'Doole

Atwood O'Doole

CURT SMITCH
Director

STATE OF WASHINGTON

DEPARTMENT OF WILDLIFE

600 Capitol Way North ● *Olympia, Washington 98501-1091*

June 26, 1992

Atwood O'Doole
6857 Bothwell Road
Reseda CA 91335

Dear Mr. O'Doole:

Director Smitch has referred your letter to me for response. Please accept my apology for the delay in answering your questions.

The type of family competition you described in your letter is not considered by this department to be a "contest". In keeping with the O'Doole tradition enjoy your fishing together and may the best man win!

Sincerely,

Bruce Crawford
Assistant Director
Fisheries Management Division

BC:dht

cc: Curt Smitch

Atwood O'Doole
6857 Bothwell Road
Reseda, California 91335

================================

May 29, 1992

Alpine Land Company
220 East First Street
Cle Elum, Washington 98922

Dear Sir/Madam:

    My name is Atwood O'Doole. In addition to owning an awning
and canopy company (O'Doole's Awning & Canopy) I am also an avid
fisherman. I'm taking my son A.J., who just turned 16, on a
special fishing trip next month in honor of Father's day and his
imminent leap into manhood. I invited Janine "Northern Exposure"
Turner to come along too. She sent me a nice photo but didn't
say anything about fishing. Maybe we'll see her when we get up
there.

    Since many of life's most precious moments are spontaneous,
I strongly feel that this should be a trip that is in no way
structured. We simply plan on traveling wherever the wind takes
us, stopping at every lake and stream along the way. I have a
very good tent which I designed and made myself. That tent will
be our home for two weeks.

    I understand that you service the entire county of Kittitas,
an area in which we will most likely pass. Do you mind if we
pitch my tent on one or more of your properties during our visit?
I'd be happy to pay you for this privilege and I promise we'll
clean up before we leave. Please let me know as soon as
possible.

                          Very truly yours,

                          Atwood O'Doole

                          Atwood O'Doole

Alpine Land Company

220 E. 1st, Cle Elum, WA 98922

Mr. Atwood O'Doole
6857 Bothwell Road
Reseda CA 91335

Dear Mr. O'Doole:

We are in receipt of your May 29th letter telling about your proposed trip to this area. While we appreciate the purpose of your trip and the desire for spontaneous activities, we are not in a position to grant permission for you to camp on any property we may represent for our sellers. Property owners wishing to sell their property contract with Realtors to sell the property only. I could anticipate that a property owner's liability could be tremendous in the event of a fire or injury, etc. We thus cannot grant permission to camp.

There are several fine campgrounds in this county that would provide the convenience of water and other useful facilities.

Best wishes for a fun time with your son.

Sincerely,

Bonnie Granger
Broker

Atwood O'Doole
6857 Bothwell Road
Reseda, California 91335

June 1, 1992

Glondo's Sausage Company
216 East First Street
Cle Elum, Washington 98922

Dear Mr. Glondo:

My name is Atwood O'Doole. In addition to owning an awning
and canopy company (O'Doole's Awning & Canopy) I am also a beef
jerky fanatic. Your ad in the Upper Kittitas County Visitor's
Guide is quite a mouth watering image. "The Best Jerky in the
Pacific Northwest" is quite a claim to live up to. I look
forward to sampling your stock when I bring my son A.J. (16) to
your area on a special Father's Day fishing excursion later this
month.

We're going to be free floating across Washington with no
itinerary, no reservations, no plans whatsoever. Just the bare
essentials -- bait, tackle, sunscreen, twinkies, Dr. Pepper,
dental floss and a tent. Do you have a lawn in front of your
store? If so, could we camp out for a night or two? I promise
we'll buy plenty of jerky and, as your ad says -- "all-meat
wieners". I'd really like to know what's in your "no-meat
wieners" before I try them though.

And if that isn't enough, I'll customize an awning just for
you. I'll make it out of "all-meat" jerky! We're going to start
packing in a few days so please get back to me on this as soon as
possible.

Very truly yours,

Atwood O'Doole

Atwood O'Doole

Glondo's Sausage Company

'Best Jerky in the Pacific Northwest'

Pacific Northwest Magazine
Dining Out Issue - 1990

HOMEMADE
Pepperoni - Italian Sausage
Smoked Kielbasa
Dry Italian Salami
All-Meat Wieners
Marinated Steak
Party & Picnic Trays
674-5755

216 East First Street - Cle Elum, WA 98922

Dear Mr O'Doole

Thankyou For you letter-
We sincirdy belive our products
are some of the finest quality
and populaity in the Northwest.

The space you requested
to camp is not appropeiate
and we know you under
stand.

Thankyou again for your
letter and interest in trying
Beg Jerky + products.

Sincerly

Charles Mondo

YAKIMA. WA 989
PM
1 JUL
1992

29 USA

Atwood O'Doole
6857 Bathwell Road
Reseda, California 91335

6857 Bothwell Rd.
Reseda, CA 91335

June 6, 1992

Mayor Tom Bradley
City Hall
200 N. Spring Street
Rm. 305
Los Angeles, CA 90010

Dear Mayor Bradley:

My name is A.J. O'Doole. My father owns an awning and
canopy company (O'Doole's Awning & Canopy) and he thinks
I'm going to work for him when I graduate next year.
He's very stubborn, just like Daryl Gates. But the Bill
of Rights says I have the freedom to choose my own
destiny so I know there must be some way out of this.

Since you've had so much experience with stubborness I'd
really like your advice. How can I choose my own
destiny?

Sincerely,

A.J. O'Doole

A.J. O'Doole

P.S. -- I think it would be neet to be a mayor. Did you
have to go to college?

September 18, 1992

Mr. A.J. O'Doole
6857 Bothwell Road
Reseda, CA 91335

Dear Mr. O'Doole:

Thank you for your letter requesting my advice on your decision to choose your own career, and inquiring about my job as Mayor.

I'm sure your father must have good intentions for wanting you to start out working in his shop, and possibly following in his footsteps to run the family business someday. As you near graduation and discover the options and goals you have for a career, you may wish to share these views with your father. You might suggest to him that you want the chance to pursue your personal dreams and desires at first, and that you need his support to do so.

Being Mayor of the nation's second largest city is very challenging, but I enjoy it. The opportunity to serve the citizens of our fine city and having the satisfaction of seeing us prosper is what this position is all about. With regard to your question about college, I feel very fortunate to have graduated from UCLA and obtain a degree in law from Southwestern College of Law. My student years, as well as time served in the Los Angeles Police Department, and experience as a City Councilman, helped prepare me for my most fulfilling role ever--Mayor.

I appreciate your having taken the time to write, and best wishes with your future endeavors.

Sincerely,

TOM BRADLEY
Mayor

TB:jk

6857 Bothwell Rd.
Reseda, CA 91335

June 6, 1992

Chief of Police Daryl Gates
Los Angeles Police Department
150 North Los Angeles Street
Los Angeles, CA 90012

Dear Chief Gates:

My name is A.J. O'Doole and I just turned sixteen years
old. It must really be hard to have everybody trying
to tell you when to retire. My father wants me to work
in his awning and canopy company (O'Doole's Awning &
Canopy) when I get out of high school. He's putting a
lot of pressure on me, just like Tom Bradley and the
City Council are putting pressure on you. It feels
horrible doesn't it?

My attorney told me that the Bill of Rights says you
have the freedom to choose your own destiny, so hang in
there! It's not over yet! My father is planning to
drag me on some stupid fishing trip for father's day
but I hate fishing almost as much as I hate awnings and
canopies. What would you do if you were me? I'd
really like to know.

Sincerely,

A.J. O'Doole

A.J. O'Doole

P.S. -- I think it would be neet to be a policeman.
Did you have to go to college?

LOS ANGELES POLICE DEPARTMENT

DARYL F. GATES
Chief of Police

TOM BRADLEY
Mayor

P. O. Box 30158
Los Angeles, Calif. 90030

June 24, 1992

Mr. A. J. O'Doole
6857 Bothwell Road
Reseda, CA 91335

Mr. O'Doole:

Thank you for your kind letter of support. When active,
concerned, caring citizens such as yourself take the time to
write, I am reassured that my Los Angeles Police officers are
doing their job right, because service to the community is still
a top priority.

At the age of sixteen, it sounds like you've got some big
decisions to make. I've always found that honest, open
discussion works best. Try it with your dad!

I would consider it a personal favor if you would continue to
support these fine men and women, long after I retire from
service. Thank you again for writing.

Very truly yours,

DARYL F. GATES
Chief of Police

Atwood O'Doole
6857 Bothwell Road
Reseda, California 91335

==

June 7, 1992

Mr. Jon Burke
Director, Transportation
c/o Warner Bros. Pictures
4000 Warner Blvd.
Burbank, California 91522

Dear Mr. Burke:

My name is Atwood O'Doole. In addition to owning an awning
and canopy company (O'Doole's Awning & Canopy) I am also a fan of
many fine Warner Bros. pictures. My wife Polly and I work very
hard to support our three charming children. When we decide to
take them all out to a Warner Bros. movie we are always assured
of outstanding production values and quality entertainment. On
behalf of the entire O'Doole family, I thank you for helping
provide us with so much pleasure.

My son A.J.'s favorite movie of all time is BATMAN. He's a
very bright boy and he's looking forward to working for me when
he graduates from high school. He just turned sixteen and I'd
like to do something special for him. He would really love it if
you allowed him to take the Batmobile for a short drive. He's
got his license now, but if you're a little nervous I'll go with
him anyway.

I'd prefer to arrange this on a weekend but I don't know if
anyone will be at the studio. If not, you could leave the keys
under a rock or something. We wouldn't go very far. We'll
probably drive up the Pacific Coast Highway to Santa Barbara and
back. I'd be very willing to give you a security deposit and the
keys to my van if it would make you feel better.

I anxiously await your reply.

Yours truly,

Atwood O'Doole

Atwood O'Doole

P.S. Maybe you'd like to make a movie about my family and myself
some day. I think it would be very entertaining. Polly thinks I
look just like Clint Eastwood, so maybe he'd want to play me.

Jon Burke
Director of Transportation

**WARNER BROS. STUDIOS
FACILITIES**

4000 Warner Boulevard
Burbank, California 91522

October 15, 1992

Mr. Atwood O'Doole
6857 Bothwell Road
Reseda, CA 91335

Dear Mr. Atwood:

I am in receipt of your letter dated June 7, 1992.

In order that we may speak in greater detail regarding
your request, please give me a call.

Thank you for your expressed interest in the Warner Bros.
Studios.

Yours truly,

JON S. BURKE
Director Of Transportation
Warner Bros. Studios Facilities

JSB:sbk

POLLY O'DOOLE
6857 BOTHWELL ROAD
RESEDA, CA 91335

♥ ♥

June 9, 1992

Mayor Tom Bradley
City Hall
200 North Spring Street
Room 305
Los Angeles, CA 90010

Dear Mayor Bradley:

I imagine you are eagerly awaiting June 29th when Chief Gates
leaves the police force. To show you that I, too, am looking
forward to this departure, I have taken the liberty of jotting
down some lyrics to a favorite tune of mine. Please feel free to
sing it at any type of rally. It might be too nasty for pulic
use, so you'd better just have a chuckle while singing it in the
shower.

Enjoy!

Sincerely,

Polly O'Doole

Polly O'Doole

When Daryl Finally Leaves the Force
(Sung to the tune of "When Johnnie Comes Marching Home Again")

When Daryl finally leaves the Force
Hurrah, Hurrah!
We'll see what other job he warps
Hurrah, Hurrah!

As Chief he was unrestrainable
His actions were unexplainable
And we'll all feel better
When Daryl leaves the Force

****

When Daryl finally leaves the post
Hurrah, Hurrah!
I will not be his whipping-post
Hurrah, Hurrah!

I'll finally get to watch him depart
I'm thrilled we got rid of that old fart
And we'll all feel better
When Daryl leaves the post

****

When Daryl finally leaves the job
Hurrah, Hurrah!
I'll throw a party and serve kebobs
Hurrah, Hurrah!

If I ever hear he's coming back
It would be cause for a heart attack
And we'll all feel better
When Daryl leaves the job

September 3, 1992

Ms. Polly O'Doole
6857 Bothwell Road
Reseda, CA 91335

Dear Ms. O'Doole:

Thank you for sending me a copy of the whimsical lyrics to your revised version of "When Johnnie Comes Marching Home Again."

You're correct in your assumption that it is not appropriate for public use, but it will make for good shower singing!

I apologize for the delay in responding to your first letter, and appreciate your having taken the time to send me another copy.

Sincerely,

TOM BRADLEY
Mayor

TB:jk

Atwood O'Doole
6857 Bothwell Road
Reseda, California 91335

═══════════════════════════════════

June 10, 1992

Laurie Ulton-Thomas
Sleep Disorder Clinic of UCLA
710 Westwood Plaza
Room 1155 RNRC
Los Angeles, California 90024

Dear Ms. Ulton-Thomas:

My name is Atwood O'Doole. In addition to owning an awning
and canopy company (O'Doole's Awning & Canopy) I am also a light
sleeper. Unfortunately, my lovely wife Polly happens to be a
<u>heavy</u> <u>snorer</u>.

I'm going on a fishing trip with my son, A.J., tomorrow.
Besides catching our limit every day, I am also looking forward
to sleeping soundly while out of earshot of Polly's nasal
passages. When I return I must take care of this issue once and
for all. A Ms. Suzanne Richter of the American Dental
Association has suggested that I contact you for guidance.

I'd like to insert something into Polly's mouth to mute her
incessant late night reverberations. But before I start
experimenting I'd like to make sure that what I do is safe.
Could you please send me a list of nontoxic items that I could
stuff into her mouth? I'm specifically interested in household
objects like sponges, ping pong balls, old newspapers and socks.

Very truly yours,

Atwood O'Doole

Atwood O'Doole

UCLA SLEEP DISORDERS CENTER
DEPARTMENT OF NEUROLOGY
710 WESTWOOD PLAZA
LOS ANGELES, CALIFORNIA 90024-1769

30 July 1992

Mr. Atwood O'Doole
6857 Bothwell Road
Reseda, CA 91335

Dear Mr. O'Doole,

I just received your letter of June 10, 1992 and hope you had a wonderful time on your fishing trip.

I appreciate your concern about your wife's snoring. Generally when a person's bedpartner complains about snoring we are concerned about an underlying sleep-related breathing disorder such as sleep apnea. Does your wife ever pause in breathing or snort while asleep? Is she tired during the day or complain of awakening with morning headaches? Does she get drowsy while driving or fall asleep easily while watching t.v.? These are some of the symptoms of sleep apnea. We have two doctors who regularly see patients for this problem and I would be happy to schedule a consultation should this be appropriate. However, if your wife snores and has none of the above-mentioned symptoms I would refer her to one of the otolaryngologists here at UCLA. In answer to your question I am unaware of any appliance which effectively eliminates snoring. There are surgical procedures which can eliminate snoring which are 90% effective - for snoring, but which are not necessarily a cure for sleep apnea. I would be happy to discuss our program with you. Please feel free to call me.

Sincerely,

Laurie Ultan-Thomas
Administrative Assistant

POLLY O'DOOLE
6857 BOTHWELL ROAD
RESEDA, CA 91335

June 11, 1992

Chief of Police Daryl Gates
Los Angeles Police Department
150 North Los Angeles Street
Los Angeles, CA 90012

Dear Chief Gates:

In order to cheer you up over your impending departure from the
Los Angeles Police Department, I have written a song for you.
You can use it whenever you want to show what has happened to
this City due to improper leadership (get my drift?).

Please enjoy the lyrics. If you're interested in background
music to sing along with, I picked up "Downtown" and four other
songs by Petula Clark at The Singing Store (corner of Victory and
Balboa - open 10:00 a.m. - 6:00 p.m. weekdays) for $12.95.

Can you please tell me if you will be signing your book at any
stores in the near future? I would love to have an autographed
copy of your book.

I look forward to hearing from you.

Sincerely,

Polly O'Doole

Polly O'Doole

DOWNTOWN
Sung to the tune of "Downtown" by Petula Clark
Lyrics by Polly O'Doole

When you're upset and life is making you angry
You can always go - Downtown
When you've got worries starting fires in a hurry
seems to help I know - Downtown

Listen to the music from your brand new ghettoblaster
You could've had a CD too if you had looted faster
How can you lose?

The lights are much brighter there
Between the flames and the flashbulbs and video glare
Let's go
Downtown - Where all the fires burn bright!
Downtown - Where prices are just right!
Downtown - Everything's waiting for you!

****

Don't hang around and let policemen surround you
There are porno shows - Downtown
Maybe you know some little places to go
Where they fence stolen clothes - Downtown

Just listen to the rhythm of the bullets flying past you
Be thankful that the Guard was late or else they would've
gassed you - Lucky again

So maybe I'll see you there
I really need a dinette set or a brand new chair
Let's go
Downtown - Where all the fires burn bright!
Downtown - Where prices are just right!
Downtown - Everything's waiting for you!

(Instrumental)

You might find somebody kind to help and understand you
Someone who is just like you and needs a gentle hand to
carry his loot

We might make the evening news
We wanted justice for Rodney but we'll settle for shoes
Let's go
Downtown - Where all the fires burn bright!
Downtown - Where prices are just right!
Downtown - Everything's waiting for you!

LOS ANGELES POLICE DEPARTMENT

DARYL F. GATES
Chief of Police

TOM BRADLEY
Mayor

P. O. Box 30158
Los Angeles, Calif. 90030

August 21, 1992

Ms. Polly O'Doole
6857 Bothwell Rd.
Reseda, CA 91335

Dear Ms. O'Doole:

Thank you for the witty lyrics. They say the best way to cope with tragedy is by laughing about it, and you certainly have accomplished a chuckle or two.

Regarding the book signing, please contact the Los Angeles Police Revolver and Athletic Club (that's our store at the Police Academy). Their address is 1880 N. Academy Drive, near Dodger Stadium in Los Angeles. The phone number is ————————. I have done book signing up there in the past, and will do so again, although there is no firm date set at this time.

Thank you again for the song, and for your interest in reading my side of the Los Angeles Law Enforcement story.

Very truly yours,

DARYL F. GATES

6857 Bothwell Rd.
Reseda, CA 91335

June 11, 1992

Congressman Anthony Beilenson
C-US Congressman 23rd District
18401 Burbank Blvd., Ste 222
Tarzana, California 91356

Dear Mr. Beilenson:

My name is A.J. O'Doole. I'm a sixteen year old
resident of your district and I've got a lot on my
mind. I can't vote yet but I still hope you will help
me. My father is trying to get me to work in his
awning and canopy company (O'Doole's Awning & Canopy)
when I graduate from high school next year. And he's
about to drag me on a stupid father-son fishing trip in
a few days. I think he got the idea from a Hallmark
Card commercial.

I'd rather eat a can of live worms than work with
awnings and canopies or go fishing. My lawyer says the
bill of rights tells me I have the freedom to choose my
own destiny. Can you send me a copy of this bill? And
please underline the part about my destiny.

Sincerely,

A. J. O'Doole

A.J. O'Doole

P.S. -- I think it would be neet to be a congressman.
Did you have to go to college?

THE BILL OF RIGHTS AND BEYOND

A RESOURCE GUIDE

SEPTEMBER

CONGRESSMAN ANTHONY C. BEILENSON
23rd District, California

The enclosed material is forwarded in response to your recent request.

If I can be of further assistance to you, please do not hesitate to call on me.

Sincerely,

Tony Beilenson

June 20, 1992 7:13 pm

Dearest Polly:

We had a wonderful drive up. We're in a town called Cle Elum. They film Northern Exposure close by. A.J. hasn't been talking much but I think he's having a great time. He met a friend in town. They went for a walk.

8:58 pm — The sky never gets this clear back home! I wish you could see it! I hope A.J. gets back soon. His hamburger is getting cold. Tell Mo and Penny Daddy misses them!

11:15 pm — I just got back from town. I tried to call you. What are you doing out so late? Did Earl unplug the phone again? No sign of A.J. but I'm not going to worry. He's probably just playing video games somewhere. He'd hate it if he thought I was waiting up on him so I better hit the hay. Good night!

I'll try to call you again tomorrow.

Love, Atwood

P.S. When I sit real still and listen I think I can hear you snoring.

6/2?/92   3:42 AM

Dad:

I met a real neet girl. She's a tattoo artist named Electra. She's 44 and she thinks I'm very mature for my age. She read my palm. It says I'm going to own my own business someday and it won't be an awning and canopy company. She's going to show me the world and help me find my destiny. We're taking the van.

Love, A.J.

P.S. Happy Father's Day.

1-002578S174 06/22/92 ICS IPMRNCZ CSP LASA
2065237353 MGMS TDRN SEATTLE-SB WA 47 06-22 1255P PDT

▶ POLLY O'DOOLE
6857 BOTHWELL RD
RESEDA CA 91335

TRIED TO CALL. WHERE ARE YOU? BAD NEWS. AJ RAN AWAY WITH OLDER WOMAN.
TOOK VAN. I HITCHED TO SEATTLE. CALLED POLICE. THEY'RE LOOKING. DON'T
WORRY. BE HOME SOON. (BRINGING LOTS OF BEEF JERKY). ROTTEN FATHER'S
DAY. LOVE,

ATWOOD

14:56 EST

MGMCOMP

6/24/92

Mom:
Dad probably
told you I ran away with
a woman. Her Name is Electra.
She's teaching me how to give
tattoos. We saw Batman Returns
today. It was really neet. I
wish I had one of those capes.
I'll be in touch.
       A.J.

© USPS 1991

Polly O'Doole
6857 Bothwell Road
Reseda, CA
          91335

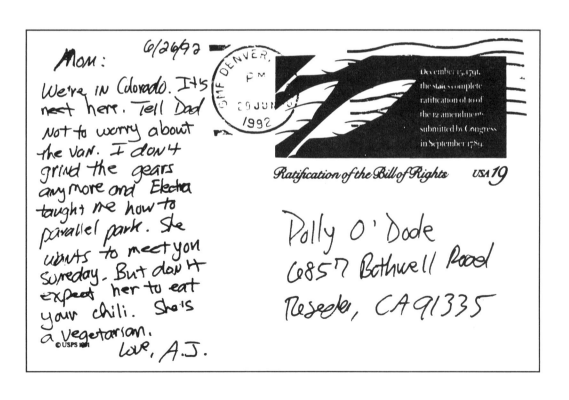

Mom: 6/26/92

We're in Colorado. It's
neet here. Tell Dad
Not to worry about
the Van. I don't
grind the gears
anymore and Electra
taught me how to
parallel park. She
wants to meet you
Someday. But don't
expect her to eat
your chili. She's
a vegetarian.
       Love, A.J.

© USPS 1991

Polly O'Doole
6857 Bothwell Road
Reseda, CA 91335

Atwood O'Doole
6857 Bothwell Road
Reseda, California 91335

═══

CONFIDENTIAL

June 27, 1992

Ms. Rosemary Watts
Dream Counselor
1114 S. Ogden Drive
Los Angeles, California

Dear Ms. Watts:

My name is Atwood O'Doole. In addition to owning an awning and canopy company (O'Doole's Awning & Canopy) I am also an emotionally troubled father and husband. While on a fishing trip in the northwest U.S. my son, A.J., 16, stole my van and ran away with a middle aged gypsy woman. As if this weren't enough, I returned home to find the rest of my family missing too!

I was beginning to think they'd all been kidnapped when my daughter Mo showed up to feed our St. Bernard, Earl. Mo told me she was staying at her friend's house while my wife Polly was in Nashville trying to sell some of her original songs. I had no idea Polly was writing songs. For God's sake, she's a junior high school cafeteria manager! She knows as much about songwriting as I do about making chili!

I feel horrible now. I thought I was in tune with my family but it appears that I've got some serious communication problems. Polly's due back in a few days, unless she makes it big -- I've been looking for her on that country music cable channel just incase. A.J. sent her a couple of postcards while on the road. I bet she's going to blame me for letting him run away.

When the entire O'Doole unit is finally reunited I want to know what to say to them and how to say it. Have you ever counseled someone in my predicament before? I can tell you that I have a recurring dream in which I am a largemouth bass trying to type a letter to Janine ("Northern Exposure") Turner on my wordprocessor but I can't because I have fins. Maybe this says something about my inability to express myself.

Please let me know what you could possibly do to help. I anxiously await your reply.

Yours truly,

Atwood O'Doole

Atwood O' Doole

P.S. -- Is your office located near the bus line?

1114 South Ogden Drive
Los Angeles, CA 90019

July 21, 1992

Mr. Atwood O'Doole
6857 Bothwell Road
Reseda, CA 91335

Dear Mr. O'Doole,

Thank you for your letter dated June 26th which I just
received in today's mail. I have had many opportunities to work
with others who have had various communication difficulities. I
appreciate your honesty in the letter, and with your sincerity
about wanting to address these sensitive and painful issues.

Enclosed is my brochure about Dream Counseling, and a short
bio on my approach and background. I am available for one-on-one
counseling. These sessions are 1½ hours in length and there is
usually time to cover up to three different dreams, depending on
the complexity of each dream. Each session is $50.00.

I feel that Dream Counseling is the best type of therapy
available because it accesses the individual's circumstances at the
root of each issue. Dreams do not lie or try to sugar coat the
problems. Through Dream Counseling, an individual can learn to
understand what is the basic concern behind each matter and
appropriate ways to deal with the problem. This kind of wisdom and
insight would normally take a great deal of time in traditional
types of therapy. However, through Dream Counseling, the problems
and solutions are presented through each dream, and help can be
readily accessed. The dream shares what is most appropriate for
that individual to know regarding any particular situation.

Since you have already had one particular dream which seems to
address your main concerns and problems, I feel confident that
Dream Counseling could aid you in understanding and discovering the
solutions your dreams are presenting. With the varied background
and approaches I utilize in these one-on-one sessions, I feel sure
that we could figure out the most appropriate solution for your
troubles.

Please contact me and we will set up an appointment. I am located two blocks off of a main bus line which should aide in your ability to come to my home office. I look forward to hearing from you in the near future and working with to address the issues you shared in your letter.

Sincerely,

Rosemary Watts

Rosemary Watts
Dream Counselor

ROSEMARY WATTS
DREAM COUNSELOR

June 28, 1992

Atwood & Polly O'Toole
6857 Bothwell Road
Reseda, CA 91335

Dear Fellow Earth Inhabitants:

Through mutual desire, your son and I have embarked on a mystic journey designed for lightworkers who are sincerely interested in interaction with the energies for the purpose of planetary healing.

We spent a brief time in Colorado releasing old programming on a cellular level, healing old wounds and merging with our Higher Selves. The next aspect of our joint exploration of the Universal Truth will take us to a geographic location conducive to natural dolphin encounters.

My relationship with your son transcends time, space and age. I am old enough to be his mother and young enough to be his daughter.

Atwood, Polly -- Identify & embrace your Karma! Love yourselves & learn to harness your anger.

BE HERE IN THE NOW!!

E

Mom: 6/29/92

Greetings from the Country
Music capital of the world!
We went to the Grand Ole
Opry. If you were here
you'd really think it was
neat. I bought you a
gift. It's a guitar shaped
oven mitt. Elektra says
hello. She saw my aura
today. It's blue. A.J.
P.S. I think I saw Garth
Brooks at Dunkin Donuts.

December 15, 1791,
the states complete
ratification of 10 of
the 12 amendments
submitted by Congress
in September 1789.

Ratification of the Bill of Rights

USPS

Polly   O'Doole
6857   Bothwell Road
Roseda, CA 91335

June 29, 1992

Pauline Gregory
656 St. George Ave.
Woodbridge, New Jersey 07095

Dear Pauline:

I'm in Nashville! Don't breathe a word of this to anyone, not even Mom. I just wanted you to know in case I die "on the road." This way I won't end up on "Unsolved Mysteries." But if I did, I trust you would provide the network with the best available picture of me.

Atwood took A.J. to Washington State on a fishing trip. It's the first of what Atwood confessed he hopes to be an annual outing for the two of them. Atwood has become mildly obsessed with passing his company along to A.J. A.J. is so young and doesn't understand the importance of it. Frankly, neither do I! Maybe Atwood is going through some sort of mid-life crisis. Anyway, after spending two weeks together, they should come up with some sort of solution. No matter what happens, I know that A.J. will show his dad the love and respect he deserves. He is a remarkable young man.

Maureen is staying at a friend's house this week so she can look after Earl. Penny is with me. Why Nashville? I think a songwriting career might be in my future. I'm taking advantage of the fishing trip because I don't think Atwood would approve. He won't be near a phone for 2 weeks. I'll be back soon unless I sign a contract and they want me to stay in Nashville!

Love,
Polly

P.S. I'm so guilt-ridden that I actually thought I saw Atwood's van drive through downtown Nashville!

© CURT TEICH & CO., INC.

July 1, 1992

Dear Mom, Dad, "Mo" and Penny,
I hope all of you aren't
worried about me. Electra
gave me a new name. From
now on I'm Honeychops.
She says it captures my
essence better than A.J.
I'm expecting some mail. Don't
open it! I'll tell you where
to forward it later.

Love,
Honeychops

Post Card

Atwood and
Polly O'Doole
6857 Bothwell Road
Reseda, CA 91335

I still can't believe what's going on around here. First A.J. disappears & now mom's gone off to get "discovered" in Nashville. When will she "discover" that she's not a long-lost Judd? The only thing missing is her link to reality. MD

By The Time You Get to Nashville - by Mo O'Doole

By the time you get to Nashville will you remember why you went? Will you remember why you think your songwriting talent's heaven sent?

By the time you get to Reseda will you remember me or dad? Cause if you forgot us or where you lived it wouldn't be so bad!

(mom- in case you ever read this remember it's a direct consequence of your insistence on rhyming!)

2:58 PM - mom's back! She and dad are having a fight. I have to go open my door so I can hear it!

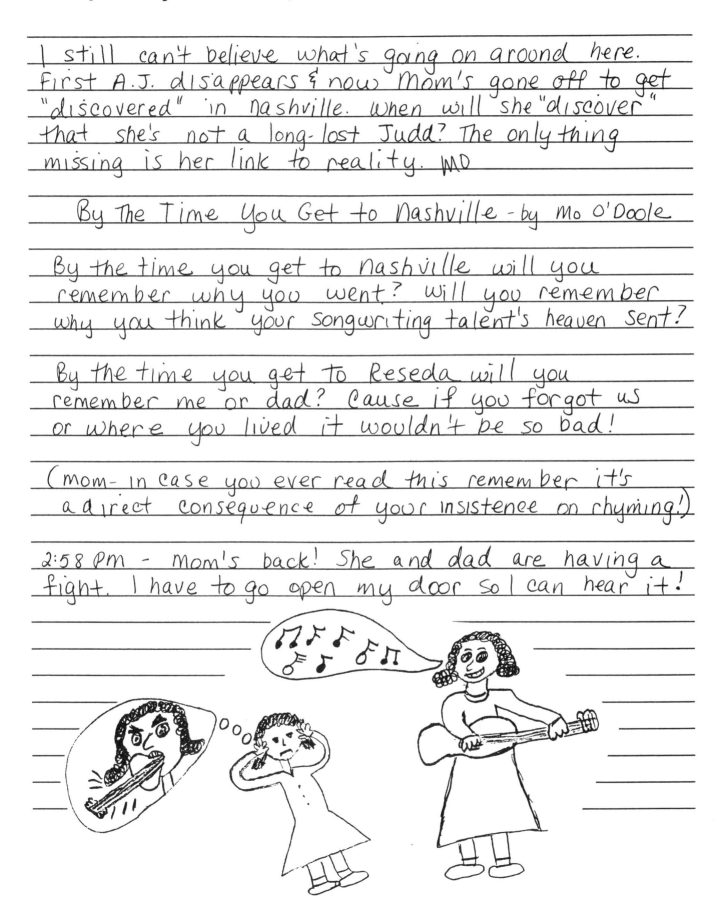

Atwood O'Doole
6857 Bothwell Road
Reseda, California 91335

===

July 6, 1992

Language Research Service
Merriam-Webster Inc.
Attn: Susan L. Brady
P.O. Box 281
Springfield, Massachusetts 01102

Dear Ms. Brady:

     My name is Atwood O'Doole. In addition to owning my own
awning and canopy company (O'Doole's Awning and Canopy) I am also
a proud owner of a Webster's Ninth New Collegiate Dictionary. My
wife Polly and I are prolific letter writers. I don't know what
we'd do without our Webster's to turn to when we need the correct
spelling of that all important adjective or we're searching for a
really good multi-syllabic noun.

     We have three charming children, one infant and two
teenagers. As you might know, young people often create their
own special lingo in order to strengthen their relationships with
one another and distance themselves from their fuddy-duddy
parents. Nevertheless, Polly and I have always made an attempt
to "schwing" and "hurl" with the younger generation.

     We have recently come across a new youth-word which we can't
find amongst the 160,000 entries in the Ninth Edition, nor in any
recent motion picture or television show. Can you please search
your files and let us know what on earth "honeychops" means?

     I anxiously await your reply.

                         Very truly yours,

                         Atwood O'Doole

                         Atwood O'Doole

Merriam-Webster Inc.
America's first publisher of dictionaries
and fine reference books.

July 30, 1992

Mr. Atwood O'Doole
6857 Bothwell Road
Reseda, CA 91335

Dear Mr. O'Doole:

   Your recent letter to Susan Brady has been directed to me for reply.
I was not surprised to come away empty-handed when I searched our files for
honeychops. Teen slang is usually marked by a short life span and a small
geographical range. A word like honeychops tends to die out before it has
a chance to make it into print, and, needless to say, such a local word is
not current among the teens of this area. Therefore, I also have no idea
what on earth honeychops means.

   As for your attempts to "'schwing' and 'hurl' with the younger generation,"
let me advise you not to try doing both simultaneously.

                              Sincerely,

                              Jennifer S. Goss

                              Jennifer S. Goss

JSG/gb

Atwood O'Doole
6857 Bothwell Road
Reseda, California 91335

July 6, 1992

Dr. Marty Scharf
c/o Mercy Hospital
Sleep Disorder Center
1275 East Kemper Road
Cincinnati, Ohio 45246

Dear Dr. Scharf:

My name is Atwood O'Doole. In addition to owning my own
awning and canopy company (O'Doole's Awning and Canopy) I am also
the spouse of a chronic snorer. While eating my cornflakes with
bananas this morning I happened to catch your interview with
Katie Couric on the Today Show. Katie's very good, isn't she? I
have her autographed picture hanging in my office. Is she as
cute and perky in person?

This so called "snoreball" you spoke of that you pin to the
back of the snorer's shirt so they won't roll over sounds good,
but what if my wife Polly cannot sleep on her stomach? And as
far as the "mouthpiece" goes I have been researching the
possibility of certain oral muffling devices myself but in my
heart of hearts I'm afraid to stuff foreign objects into any of
my better half's orifices.

My van was recently stolen so I've been spending a lot of
time at home tinkering in my garage. I recently put together
something which you might be very interested in. I call it the
"O'Doole Snore Box" :

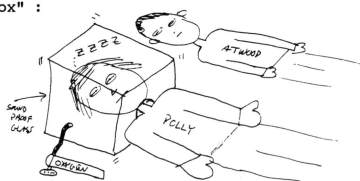

With the head of the snorer snugly inserted into this sound
proof chamber, the snorer is free to roll over and there is no
danger of choking. If you want I can send you a model to try out
on your patients then if you're interested maybe we could make a
deal. I look forward to hearing from you.

Very truly yours,

Atwood O'Doole

Atwood O'Doole

The Center For Research In Sleep Disorders

Martin B. Scharf, Ph.D., A.C.P., Director

December 16, 1992

A. O'Doole
6857 Bathwell Way
Roceda, CA 91335

Dear Mr. O'Doole:

I received your letters and I apologize for not responding. We
do not have any interest in your snore box at this time. Our
primary interest is in Obstructive Sleep Apnea Syndrome and our
involvement with snoring itself is simply peripheral.

Wishing you good luck in your endeavors.

Sincerely,

Martin B. Scharf, Ph.D., A.C.P.
Director

MBS/drr

POLLY O'DOOLE
6857 BOTHWELL ROAD
RESEDA, CA 91335

July 8, 1992

Creative Artist Agency
9830 Wilshire Boulevard
Beverly Hills, CA 90212-1825
Attn: <u>Lori Anderson</u>

Dear Ms. Anderson:

A recent trip to Nashville to fulfill my dream of becoming a
songwriter proved to be quite unsuccessful. I didn't really
make the proper appointments with agents or managers before I
left California. I figured the spirits of all those great
country western singers/songwriters would lead me down the path
to fame and fortune or at least open a few doors for me.
Unfortunately, every time I opened my mouth to sing a verse or
two to someone, they just stared at me. I think I'm an OK singer
but not good enough to render a fan speechless! My talent lies
in my songwriting ability.

Needless to say, I left Nashville a pretty devastated woman. But
not nearly as devastated as when I found out that while I was
gone, my sixteen year-old son, A.J., ran off with a forty-four
year-old woman! I believe this experience has given me a the
feeling of rock-bottom hopelessness that is oh so vital to a good
country western tune.

I enclose the lyrics to "My Young Son Ran Off With a Woman" for
your consideration. I would appreciate it if you would be able
to sell this song for me. Please let me know if you are
interested.

Thank you.

Polly O'Doole
Polly O'Doole

[NO RESPONSE]

MY YOUNG SON RAN OFF WITH A WOMAN
Sung to the tune of "My Bonnie Lies Over the Ocean"
Lyrics by Polly O'Doole

My young son ran off with a woman
A woman who's older than me
If I'm not mistaken kidnappin'
Is considered a felony

    Bring back, bring back
    Oh bring back my A.J. to me, to me
    Bring back, bring back
    Oh bring back my A.J. to me

My husband took our son out fishin'
He thought that perhaps they would bond
What my Atwood did not envision
Is with his van our son would abscond

    Bring back, bring back
    Oh bring back my Chevy to me, to me
    Bring back, hubcaps intact
    Oh bring back my van to me

They drove from Seattle to Nashville
Without cash you'd think it'd be hard
But really it was oh so simple
Cause A.J. "borrowed" dad's credit card

    Bring back, bring back
    Oh bring back my Visa to me, to me
    You kleptomaniac
    Oh bring back my Visa to me

I'm not throwing stones - I'm just sayin'
From now on leave minors alone
If you are so fond of young children
Give birth to a few of your own

    Bring back, bring back
    Bring back A.J., not some "Honeychop"
    You nymphomaniac
    Then all charges I will drop!

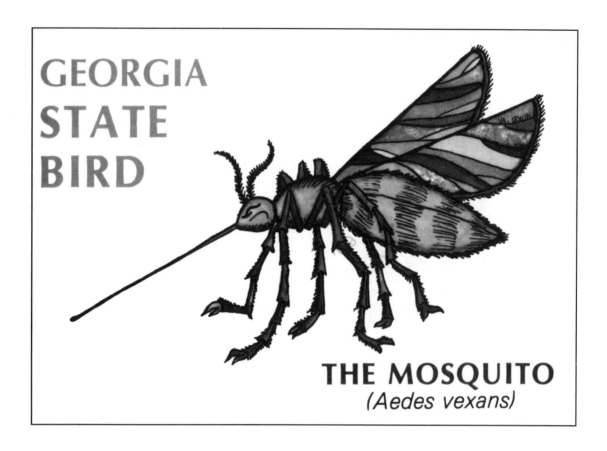

GEORGIA
STATE
BIRD

THE MOSQUITO
(Aedes vexans)

July 17, 1992

Dear family:

This journey is evolving into a consciousness expanding event. We've been meditating and eating birdseed for the last two weeks. Electra has helped me cut all ties to the physical world. I am finally attuning to my inner self. I sense greatness on the horizon.

With you in spirit,
Honeychops

GA Scenic South, Box 14, Pell City, Alabama 35128

NORTH METRO GA 3015
PM
1992

POST CARD

THE O'DOOLE'S
6857 Bothwell Rd.
Reseda, CA 91335

P335048
© Plastichrome®
Printed in Ireland

KENTUCKY The Bluegrass State

**GREETINGS FROM KENTUCKY
THE BLUEGRASS STATE**

Dear MR. Dekom: 7/25/92

    Thanks for answering my questions about being a lawyer and telling me about the Bill of Rights. I'm on vacation now and I desperately need some advice. What do I have to do to legally change my name from "A.J." to "Honeychops"? Please reply to me at 6857 Bothwell Road, Reseda, CA 91335

    Thanks in advance,

Honeychops (formerly A.J. O'Doole)

BLUE GRASS SOUVENIRS, 1533 EASTLAND PARKWAY, LEXINGTON, KY 40505

post card

Peter Dekom
Bloom Dekom & Hergott
150 South Rodeo Drive
3rd Floor
Beverly Hills, CA
      90212

SPACE BELOW RESERVED FOR U.S. POSTAL SERVICE

101
L-4552-E
Printed in Canada

BLOOM, DEKOM AND HERGOTT

ATTORNEYS AT LAW

150 SOUTH RODEO DRIVE, THIRD FLOOR
BEVERLY HILLS, CALIFORNIA 90212

JACOB A. BLOOM
PETER J. DEKOM
ALAN S. HERGOTT
LAWRENCE H. GREAVES
CANDICE S. HANSON
MATTHEW G. KRANE
MELANIE COOK
TINA J. KAHN
JULIE M. PHILIPS
THOMAS F. HUNTER
JOHN D. DIEMER

STEPHEN D. BARNES
GARY L. GILBERT
STUART M. ROSENTHAL
LEIGH BRECHEEN
STEPHEN F. BREIMER
DEBORAH L. KLEIN
JONATHAN BLAUFARB
STEVEN L. BROOKMAN
LARY SIMPSON
JOHN LaVIOLETTE
ROBYN L. ROTH

THOMAS P. POLLOCK
FOUNDING PARTNER
THROUGH 1986

July 30, 1992

"Honeychops" O'Doole
6857 Bothwell Road
Reseda, CA 91335

Dear "Honeychops":

In respect of your question on how to change your name, I strongly advise using your left hand.

Please accept my best regards.

Very truly yours,

PETER J. DEKOM
of BLOOM, DEKOM and HERGOTT

PJD/rbl

GREETINGS FROM KENTUCKY
THE BLUEGRASS STATE

7/26/9

Dear Family:
   I had a vision last
week whilst communing with
wildlife in the Smoky Mountains.
Three words emblazoned across
a gigantic golden canopy:
"Sleeveless Outer Garments"
Electra says it's important.
  More to come,
     Honeychaps

© BLUE GRASS SOUVENIRS, 1533 EASTLAND PARKWAY, LEXINGTON, KY 40505

101
L-4552-E
Printed in Canada

post card

The O'Doodles
6857 Bothwell Road
Reseda, CA 91335

SPACE BELOW RESERVED FOR U.S. POSTAL SERVICE

POLLY O'DOOLE
6857 BOTHWELL ROAD
RESEDA, CA 91335

♥ ♥

July 27, 1992

Frito Lay, Inc.
7701 Legacy Drive
Plano, TX 75024
Attn: <u>Steve Reinumund, CEO</u>

Dear Mr. Reinumund:

I wanted to place an advertisement on a milk carton for a
runaway child. However, even though my son, A.J., is a minor,
he is considerably older than most of the missing children on
milk cartons.

I thought I'd write to your company to see if some of your dairy
related products like "Cheese Doodles" might carry endorsements
for missing teens. The reason I mentioned "Cheese Doodles" is
because they are an O'Doole family favorite (we call them "Cheese
O'Doodles!") yet popular with teens.

I would appreciate any assistance from you.

Sincerely,

Polly O'Doole

Polly O'Doole

 Frito-Lay, Inc.

February 25, 1993

Ms. Polly O'Doole
6857 Bothwell Drive
Reseda, CA 91335

Dear Ms. O'Doole,

Steve Reinemund received your letter and because he was travelling, he asked
that I respond to you. I'm grateful for the chance to address your very
unique request.

I am sorry to hear of your unfortunate situation and certainly wish I could be
of more assistance regarding the addition of photos to our packaging. FDA
labeling regulations, however, require that specific product information (ie.
ingredient statement, nutrition data) be printed on our packages leaving
little space for additional information. New regulations are forthcoming, but
indications are that even more information will be required. In addition,
packaging material is typically ordered in large quantities allowing us to
retain inventories for as much as two years. This makes it difficult to make
frequent packaging changes.

Ms. O'Doole, I am not familiar with the snack product you mentioned in your
letter - "Cheese Doodles". Frito-Lay's own cheese flavored snack is sold
nationwide under the name of CHEE.TOS and enclosed are a few coupons to
encourage you to try this product.

Again, I apologize for our inability to comply with your request and I wish
you much success in your search. Thank you for taking the time to contact us.

Sincerely,

Susan G. Mohel
Manager, Consumer Affairs

ENCLOSED:

(2) Free Product Coupon

FL-2300-16

POLLY O'DOOLE
6857 BOTHWELL ROAD
RESEDA, CA 91335

♥ ♥

July 29, 1992

Mr. John G. Middlebrook
General Manager
Pontiac
1 Pontiac Plaza
Pontiac, MI 48340

Dear Mr. Middlebrook:

Due to a family mishap, my husband and are forced to buy another
automobile. I want to buy "American" but am confused by the
names you and other car companies have chosen for our new
American autos.

Why name a car "Reatta," "Achieva" or "Probe"? What type of
words are these - nouns or adjectives? I understand the concept
of "Skylark" and "Mustang". You can close your eyes and see a
bird, the skylark, darting in and out of the wind. Or imagine a
wild stallion exploding with energy. These are all great word
associations for automobiles. But if someone told me they just
bought an Achieva I wouldn't know whether to congratulate them or
say "Gesundheit!!" And what do <u>you</u> see when you close your eyes
and imagine a Probe? I don't want to describe what I see! How
would you use these words in everyday conversation? "Honey, the
spaghetti and meatballs were particularly Reatta tonight!" Do
you see what I mean? These words don't stand alone. Please
don't make comparisons to Toyota non-words like "Camry", "Tercel"
and "Cressida" because the Japanese do not understand the nuances
of the English language. You should know better.

I can't say that I would purchase an automobile solely because of
its name. On the other hand, I would be hesitant to let people
know I was the owner of a new 1993 "Chevrolet Slug".

I anxiously await your Probe.

Sincerely,

Polly O'Doole

Polly O'Doole

P.S. Sometimes my meatballs <u>do</u> taste Reatta!

3/4/93

MS. POLLY O'DOOLE
6857 BOTHWELL ROAD
RESEDA, CA 91335

THANK YOU FOR YOUR LETTER OF 1/11/93 REGARDING
AUTOMOTIVE NAMES. THE PROCESS WE USE TO CHOOSE THE PROPER
VEHICLE NAMES FOR OUR PRODUCTS IS CONTROLLED BY THE PONTIAC
NAME COMMITTEE. THERE IS A PROCESS FOR CHOOSING NAMES WHICH
IS AS FOLLOWS:

- A LIST OF PROPOSED NAMES IS CHOSEN (SOME WITH
  MEANINGS, OTHERS WITHOUT MEANINGS, SOME ALPHA
  NUMERIC AND OTHERS NUMERIC)

- THIS LIST IS THEN REDUCED, BY THE PROCESS OF
  ELIMINATION, TO WHAT THE COMMITTEE FEELS ARE THE
  10 - 15 BEST NAMES

- THESE NAMES ARE THEN RESEARCHED WITH THE TARGET
  MARKET CUSTOMERS, WHO ACTUALLY GET TO LOOK AT A
  PROTOTYPE OF THE FUTURE PRODUCT

- THE PROSPECTIVE CUSTOMERS JUDGE EACH NAME ON HOW IT
  FITS WITH THE VEHICLE SHAPE AND IMAGE, WHAT EACH
  NAME MEANS TO THEM AND WHAT EFFECT THE NAME WOULD
  HAVE ON THEIR PURCHASE DECISION MAKING PROCESS.

- THE HIGHEST SCORING NAME IS TRADEMARKED AND UTILIZED
  AS THE VEHICLE NAME

DUE TO THE FACT THAT PONTIAC CARS ARE DESIGNED TO BE SPORTY,
YOUTHFUL VEHICLES ... MANY OF OUR VEHICLES ARE NAMED AFTER
RACES, RACE TRACKS OR PLACES WHERE HIGH SPEED TESTING IS
PERFORMED, SUCH AS: "TRANS AM", "LE MANS" AND "BONNEVILLE".
"GRAND AM" AND "TRANS SPORT" WERE DERIVATIVES FROM
"TRANS AM".

I HOPE THIS PROVIDES YOU WITH SOME INSIGHT AS TO HOW PONTIAC
CHOOSES NAMES FOR ITS FUTURE PRODUCTS. THANK YOU AGAIN FOR
TAKING THE TIME TO WRITE.

W.C. HEUGH
MARKETING DIRECTOR
CHAIRMAN OF NAME COMMITTEE

POLLY O'DOOLE
6857 BOTHWELL ROAD
RESEDA, CA 91335

♥ ♥

August 2, 1992

Iced Tea
c/o Warner Bros. Records
3300 Warner Boulevard
Burbank, CA 91505

Dear Mr. Tea:

I know you've been getting a lot of pressure lately from everyone
to stop singing your song "Cop Killer." On the one hand, it's
your Constitutional right to sing whatever you want. On the
other hand -- the hand that feeds you! -- you don't want to
alienate people so they'll boycott this and all future albums.
Constitutional rights or wrongs -- making money is what being
American is all about! I think I have a solution.

Keep the title "Cop Killer" on the album, but record a new
version with more upbeat lyrics. I have enclosed a sample new
version of "Cop Killer, Cop Killer" sung to the tune of
"Matchmaker, Matchmaker" from the long-running Broadway play,
"Fiddler On The Roof."

                "Cop Killer, Cop Killer"
        Sung to the Tune of "Matchmaker, Matchmaker"

                Cop Killer, Cop Killer
                Put Down Your Gun
                Let's bake some cookies
                And have us some fun

                Cop Killer, Cop Killer
                Don't be so brazen
                How 'bout oatmeal or raisin?

I think that's enough to give you an idea of this new approach.

Good luck.

Sincerely,

Polly O'Doole

Polly O'Doole

[NO RESPONSE]

POLLY O'DOOLE
6857 BOTHWELL ROAD
RESEDA, CA 91335

♥ ♥

August 2, 1992

Ms. Nancy Huonder
Law Information Officer
Minnesota Department of Natural Resources
550 Lafayette Road
St. Paul, Minnesota 55155-4047

Dear Ms. Huonder:

I understand the Minnesota Department of Natural Resources has
roadkill cookbooks with recipes for "splattered deer" and "skunk
a la tire." Can you please tell me where I can purchase one of
these cookbooks?

During the early days of our marriage, there were times when my
husband, Atwood, and I had nothing to eat but the remains of a
driving disaster. There may not have been a lot of food to pass
around in those days, but there sure were second helpings of love
and affection. The O'Dooles are having a family crisis and
Atwood feels he is to blame -- and he's right. But I'd still
like to cheer him up by reminding him of the good, old days. The
only problem is that we don't eat much meat nowadays and I
wouldn't know where to find edible roadkill. Sometimes I see a
dead pigeon on the street, but mostly the only kind of meat
you'll find lying on the freeway is a half-eaten burrito someone
threw out of their car window. Actually, I'd really like to find
recipes for fishing mishaps, although they're not traditionally
considered car kill. If someone's Jeep swirved off the road,
fell into a lake and speared a trout with their radio antennae,
would that constitute a "car kill?"

Can I sell you some of my fish recipes for a future book you
might be interested in publishing? I can make up funny names
too! Like "Halibut on a Headlight" or "Fish a la Fender Bender"
or "Grouper on my Front Grill."

Sincerely,

Polly O'Doole

Polly O'Doole

STATE OF
MINNESOTA
DEPARTMENT OF NATURAL RESOURCES

500 LAFAYETTE ROAD • ST. PAUL, MINNESOTA • 55155-40_____

December 4, 1992

Polly O'Doole
6857 Bothwell Road
Reseda, CA 91335

Dear Ms. O'Doole:

The Minnesota Department of Natural Resources, Enforcement Division is in receipt of your letter regarding roadkill cookbooks.

Unfortunately, you have been misinformed. The Division of Enforcement does not publish nor sell any type of cookbook. I would suggest checking with a larger bookstore in your area for help in obtaining such a unique book.

Your question of a Jeep's antennae spearing a trout when it swerves off a road into a lake is an interesting concept, however the fish would not be considered a roadkill, it would be a speared fish.

Thank you for your offer of recipes, however, we are not planning any publication of cookbooks.

Good luck in your search.

Sincerely,

Nancy Huonder bja

Nancy Huonder
Information Officer
Division of Enforcement

NH:bja

Greetings from Ohio

SCENIC RURAL OHIO
Often sought after and enjoyed by residents and visitors alike.
Ohio has many "get away" areas that help satisfy one's need for quiet, peaceful, natural beauty.

Lucky Prints

P M

4 AUG 1992

452

©Molloy Postcard Services, 1100 Pike Street, Covington, KY 41011

19 USA

August 3, 1992

Dear O'Dooles:
    I was led to purchase a sewing kit today. Followed a bright light to a fabric store. Beginning to understand the vision.
    Fulfilling my destiny,
        Honey chops

THE O'DOOLES
6857 Bothwell Road
Reseda, CA
        91335

POLLY O'DOOLE
6857 BOTHWELL ROAD
RESEDA, CA 91335

August 5, 1992

Kate Hutton, PhD
Caltech
252-21
Pasadena, CA 91125

Dear Dr. Hutton:

A recent article in the Los Angeles Times indicated that the
current rash of earthquakes are slowly restructuring the
geography of Southern California. I believe the article states
that Palm Springs has moved 4" to the East. I always wanted to
move my family back East, but not this way!

Our home is on the borderline of Reseda and Canoga Park. The
last time my husband and I had our house appraised, we were
told that if we lived across the street in Canoga Park (which
is a more geographically desirable location from which to sell
property), our house would be worth at least $25,000 more. How
many more earthquakes (and at what magnitudes) will it take for
nature to relocate our house 40 feet across the street to Canoga
Park? Or if the Eastward trend continues, is it possible for
Canoga Park to push itself into Reseda? If Canoga Park moves
East, will our house be in the old Reseda or the new Canoga Park?
Who decides what the boundaries are once they become structurally
changed by nature? Also, what are the chances that my house will
still be standing if the magnitude of an earthquake is strong
enough to move it across the street? Or does a move that large
happen slowly over time as a result of smaller more frequent
earthquakes?

I would appreciate it if you could get back to me soon because
your answer could help us in deciding when to sell our house.

Thank you,

Polly O'Doole

Polly O'Doole

CALIFORNIA INSTITUTE OF TECHNOLOGY

SEISMOLOGICAL LABORATORY

Polly O'Doole
6857 Bothwell Road
Reseda CA 91335

Dear Ms. O'Doole,

Sorry to take so long to answer your questions, but things have
been a little busy around here. So I'll get right to it.

Earthquakes have been known to produce offsets of 30 feet or so,
as the recent Landers quake did in the Mojave Desert. However,
this is right along the fault, from one side to the other.
In all surrounding areas, the land is deformed, but not to the
extent noticable to the naked eye. So unless a major fault runs
right through your block and a M7+ earthquake happens on that fault,
your house would not be relocated into Canoga Park. Surprisingly,
most relatively new wood-frame houses can stand up to that, as
long as the fault or any of its branches does not run right
underneath. Cosmetic cracks, chimney damage, and general
rearrangement of the contents of the house are expected, but the
house should remain structurally sound.

As to who defines city boundaries and how, I don't know the answer.
I know that the U.S./Mexico border was offset by about 6 feet in
1940, so the issue must have been addressed. It is my understanding
that the border is defined in terms of surveying monuments, so
it just ends up with a dog-leg in it. Interesting question.

Kate Hutton
Kate Hutton
Staff Seismologist

**POLLY O'DOOLE
6857 BOTHWELL ROAD
RESEDA, CA 91335**

August 12, 1992

Marcia Braunstein
c/o Golden Boot Awards
23300 Ventura Boulevard
Woodland Hills, CA 91364

Dear Ms. Braunstein:

Attached is a copy of your flyer for the Tenth Annual Golden Boot
Awards which is being held this Saturday, August 15, 1992. I
only saw the flyer today in the supermarket and cannot possibly
attend on such short notice. I would appreciate it if you could
keep my address on your mailing list for next year's ceremony.

Since I do not recognize some of the names of this year's
honorees, am I correct in assuming that some honorees are just
plain folk, not movie stars? I am curious to know what someone
has to do to become an honoree of the Golden Boot Award. My
husband, Atwood, is an outdoorsman and has been known on occasion
to stay up into the wee hours of the morning watching reruns of
some of the great cowboy movies of yore. Sometimes after a six-
pack and a night of "Hoot Gibson" and "Tex Ritter," I have to
"boot his golden butt" up the stairs!

Atwood is also the owner of an awning and canopy company
(O'Doole's Awnings and Canopy) and is in the middle of what I
believe to be a "mid-life crisis." It sure would cheer him up to
be an honoree at the Golden Boot Awards Ceremony of 1993. Please
let me know if you'll consider my request.

Sincerely,

Polly O'Doole

Polly O'Doole

P.S. Please address all correspondence to me, not my husband.
     I want this to be a big surprise!

MOTION
PICTURE &
TELEVISION
FUND

November 20, 1992

Mrs. Polly O'Doole
6857 Bothwell Road
Reseda, CA   91335

Dear Polly,

Thank you for your letter that I received November 17. I notice it was dated August 12. I am sorry but as far as I am aware, it was not received in this office. I hope this delay did not cause you any inconvenience.

To answer your question about the honorees, the Golden Boot Awards honor individuals who have contributed a great deal to Western films . . . the cowboy stars, cowgirls, directors, writers, character actors and stuntpeople. I hope this helps.

I will be happy to add your name to the mailing list for the 11th Annual Golden Boot Awards. Mark your calendar for Saturday, August 28.

I have enclosed a copy of the 10th Annual Award book so you can see the background of the honorees.

Sincerely,

Marcia K. Braunstein

Marcia K. Braunstein
Manager, Donor Programs

MKB/pab

Enclosure

Golden Boot
Awards

AUGUST 15, 1992

THE CENTURY PLAZA HOTEL AND TOWER

*Special 10th Anniversary
Commemorative Edition*

MOTION
PICTURE &
TELEVISION
FUND

POLLY O'DOOLE
6857 BOTHWELL ROAD
RESEDA, CA 91335

August 14, 1992

Mr. Phil Donahue
c/o "Donahue"
W-NBC
30 Rockefeller Plaza, 8th Floor
New York, New York 10112

Dear Phil:

Until recently, I thought my family was "normal." My husband,
Atwood, owns his own awning and canopy company. I work in the
cafeteria at our local junior high school. The behavior of our
three children, A.J. (16), Maureen (13) and Penny (2) have never
been cause for alarm. Recent developments in my family life have
changed dramatically. My husband, Atwood, and I are loath to
admit that our sixteen year-old son, A.J., has run off with a
forty-four year old woman. They stole my husband's van while
Atwood took A.J. on a special fishing trip in the Pacific
Northwest and are on a cross-country joyride. The last time we
heard from A.J., he was in Ohio. You'll notice I do not use her
name because I refuse to refer to this woman other than in
epithets.

In light of the recent Woody Allen scandal, I thought some of the
talk shows might be doing May-December or December/May romance
stories. This feels more like an April/October situation. April
for "April Fool's Day" and October for "Halloween." It's kind of
a joke and a nightmare all rolled into one.

Please let me know if you need me as a guest. My husband,
Atwood, might want to talk too. By the way, he and I are the
same age.

Sincerely,

Polly O'Doole

Polly O'Doole

Dear DONAHUE Correspondent:

Because of the great volume of mail received in our office, we're sorry we cannot answer your letter personally. We are keeping your idea on file.

Your suggestion has been reviewed. However, we do not plan to use your idea for a DONAHUE program.

Thank you for your interest in our show.

                    THE DONAHUE STAFF

DONAHUE
30 Rockefeller Plaza
New York, N.Y. 10112

NEW YORK
OCT - 1 '92
N.Y.

U.S.POSTAGE
0.19

Polly O'Doole
6857 Bothwell Road
Reseda, CA 91335

CAPITOL BUILDING
Washington, D.C.

8/22/92

Dear Mom: Remember ~~that~~ the
old sewing machine in the garage?
Don't throw it away! It's an
important part of _my_ future.
Dear Dad: How would you like to
invest $5,000 in a new business?
It's going to be the next big
thing. I promise!
    Soon to be rich,
       Honey chaps

Photo: David Noble, Plastichrome ©

INC. WASHINGTON, D.C. 20005

POST CARD

Polly & Atwood
       O'Doole
6857 Bothwell Road
Reseda, CA 91335

Aerial view of the fabulous Atlantic City skyline. In this view, the ocean, beach and casinos are seen.

September 3, 1992

Dear Dad: Great news! I don't need your money and I'm coming home soon! I put my last dollar in a slot machine and won $20,000! I bought you a new van and I'm using the rest to start my own business "Honeychops' House of Capes". Electra says I'm going to make a fortune! See you in a few days! Honeychops

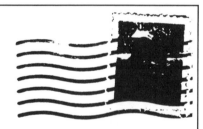

POST CARD
Address

Atwood O'Doole
6857 Bothwell Road
Reseda, CA
91335

Atwood O'Doole
6857 Bothwell Road
Reseda, California 91335

═══

September 7, 1992

President George Herbert Walker Bush
The White House
1600 Pensylvania Avenue
Washington D.C. 20500

Dear President Bush:

My name is Atwood O'Doole. In addition to owning my own
awning and canopy company (O'Doole's Awning and Canopy) I am also
a true believer in "family values". My lovely wife Polly and my
three charming children are my pride and joy. Nevertheless, we
do have problems sometimes. Like this summer when my oldest,
A.J., stole my van and ran away with an older woman named
Electra. For weeks we didn't know if we were ever going to see
him again. But, our prayers were answered when he recently
informed us that he is on his way back to Reseda.

To celebrate this very special homecoming we're having a
"Welcome Home A.J." party on Monday, September 14. I'd like to
officially invite you to attend. And feel free to make a speech
if you want. We're still undecided voters so it might be worth
your time. Polly will be serving her irrestible homemade chili,
A.J.'s going to christen my new van and my daughter Maureen
("Mo") is going to give us a rare treat and read one of her
original poems.

If you want to spend the night I can put a couple of cots in
the garage and make it real comfy for you and Barb. Since you're
not used to Polly's snoring, you're better off out there anyway.

Please let us know right away whether you can make it. Feel
free to bring Dan and Marilyn too!

Very truly yours,

Atwood O'Doole

Atwood O'Doole

September 16, 1992

Dear Mr. O'Doole:

On behalf of the President, thank you for your recent
invitation.

You were very kind to extend this opportunity to the President.
Unfortunately, due to an already heavily committed schedule he
was unable to accept your invitation. However, he has asked me
to convey to you his appreciation for your thoughtfulness and
his best wishes.

                    Sincerely,

                    Katherine L. Super

                    KATHERINE L. SUPER
                    Deputy Assistant to the President
                    for Appointments and Scheduling

Mr. Atwood O'Doole
6857 Bothwell Road
Reseda, CA 91335

My Diary   September 14, 1992

A.J. finally returned to Reseda. Not quite as poetic as the swallows returning to San Juan Capistrano, but it's nice to have someone else for Dad to get mad at. He brought a friend with him. Her name is Electra. I can't put my finger on it at the moment, but something just isn't right. First of all, she's older than mom but she's definitely cooler. She's very mystical. I bet she was a real hippie in the 60's. I think I'm going to like her. If only I could figure out why she likes my brother. Dad's ecstatic that his prodigal son has returned. Today was the big welcome home bash. In horor of A.J.'s newfound independence. I penned the following: Mo

           Hurry Up and Cut the Umbilical Cord
                  by Mo O'Doole

      Hurry Up and Cut the Umbilical Cord
      So I may rumble, tumble, stumble independently
      through life's esoteric jokes
           Worrying, flurrying, scurrying to fit it
           all into one lifetime

      Hurry Up and pull the plug
      So I may dream, scheme, scream
      Once I am cognizant of the punchlines
           Sighing, Lying, Crying that it's over before I was
      ready.

Dad said he was glad the President didn't show up and hear my poem.

Atwood O'Doole
6857 Bothwell Road
Reseda, California 91335

September 17, 1992

Mr. Jimmy Stewart
P.O. Box 90
Beverly Hills, California 90213

Dear Mr. Stewart:

My name is Atwood O'Doole. In addition to owning my own awning and canopy company (O'Doole's Awning and Canopy) I am also one of your biggest fans. As a family driven, working class, earnest American, I feel quite akin to your image in movies like IT'S A WONDERFUL LIFE. I want to personally thank you for creating characters I can relate to which have given me so much pleasure and inspiration over the years.

I recently had a dream that an angel, who looked just like Janine ("Northern Exposure") Turner, showed me what life would have been like if I never existed. I saw my wife Polly in a Beverly Hills mansion, married to a wealthy shades and blinds tycoon. My son A.J. was the world's first sixteen year old brain surgeon. My daughter Mo was an Olympic gold medal winning swimmer. The Dodgers won the World Series. The L.A. Riots never happened. Zero percent unemployment. All diseases could be cured. There was global peace.

Needless to say, I awoke feeling like I didn't matter at all. You see, it's been a bad year in the O'Doole home. My son A.J. ran away this past summer. I was tickled to death when he finally came home this week. But I was shocked that he brought his forty four year old girlfriend with him. Right now, I'm making her sleep in the garage. Do you think this is the right thing to do? She has no home and very little money. I can't just throw her out in the street, or can I?

I just keep wondering what George Bailey of IT'S A WONDERFUL LIFE would do in this situation. If you have any wisdom to impart I'd love to hear it. If not, I'd settle for an autographed picture.

Very truly yours,

Atwood O'Doole

Atwood O'Doole

Atwood O'Doole
6857 Bothwell Road
Reseda, California 91335

===

October 6, 1992

Mr. Dave Powell
Husbandry Department
Monterey Bay Aquarium
886 Cannery Row
Monterey, California 93940-4888

Dear Mr. Powell,

My name is Atwood O'Doole. In addition to owning an awning
and canopy company (O'Doole's Awning & Canopy) I also have three
wonderful children (A.J., 16, Mo, 13, Penny, 3), and a lovable
Saint Bernard (Earl, 14 in dog years). The kids and I recently
got my lovely wife Polly an aquarium for her birthday. But we
don't have any fish to put in it.

All the pet stores I have visited only carry small exotic
frilly looking things. I'm not even sure some of them are fish!
I want this to be an educational experience for my family. I
don't want them to get the impression that America's lakes and
streams are populated by these tiny bright colored swimming
Christmas ornaments. They should experience the beauty of <u>real</u>
fish, just like the ones I used to catch back in Kansas. Perhaps
you've got some extras of these in your own aquarium. If so, can
I buy a couple from you?

In particular, I'd like an Ictalurus Punctatus (Channel
Catfish) and a Micropterus salmoides (Largemouth Bass) I'm not
sure about the integration of these species. Can an Ictalurus
Punctatus live with a Micropterus salmoides? I'd hate to see
these guys fighting like cats and dogs. Also, if they get too
big and I don't want to get another aquarium, which one(s) make
the best fish sticks?

I also need to know what they eat. What about table scraps?
No bones or anything. I'm thinking leftover chili or peaches
chopped up real fine.

I can assure you that I will follow any guidelines necessary
to keep your fish healthy and contented. Despite a few recent
incidents, we're a very happy, well adjusted family and I think
we'd make a fine home for any future pets (just ask Earl!).

I look forward to hearing from you.

Yours truly,

Atwood O'Doole

Atwood O'Doole

MONTEREY BAY AQUARIUM

December 14, 1992

Atwood O'Doole
6857 Bothwell Road
Reseda, CA 91335

Dear Atwood,

Please forgive the lateness of my reply to your letter. I have
been out of town for sometime.

You did not mention the size of the aquarium you gave to your
wife but unless it is quite large I do not recommend keeping
largemouth bass and channel catfish. They both grow rapidly to a
large size and are both aggressive.

If you have not had any experience with aquariums I suggest that
you begin with some inexpensive, hardy small fishes from your
local aquarium store. They can recommend some and a book on how
to care for them.

Incidentally, we do not have bass or catfish in our aquarium. We
only exhibit native California fishes and they are originally
form east of the Rockies.

Good luck to you, your family and Earl.

Sincerely,

David C. Powell
Director of Husbandry

DCP:tb

POLLY O'DOOLE
6857 BOTHWELL ROAD
RESEDA, CA 91335

October 29, 1992

"Unsolved Mysteries"
4303 West Verdugo Avenue
Burbank, CA 91505
Attn: <u>Tim Rogan, Coordinating Producer</u>

Dear Mr. Rogan:

I would appreciate it very much if you could share with me some
of the tactics you employ while trying to uncover information
about someone.

My husband, Atwood, and I are reluctantly hosting "America's Most
Unwanted" houseguest. Atwood took our son, A.J. on a fishing
trip in Washington. A.J. met a woman older than me who convinced
him to abandon his father, "borrow" his father's van and go on a
cross-country spree with her. A.J. has since come to his senses
and returned home. Unfortunately, he brought this woman with him
and she is currently living in our garage. We know very little
about her but what we do know is suspicious.

     1.   First of all, her name is "Electra."   She doesn't use
a surname -- just "Electra." How do I find out her real name?

     2.   She has several tatoos on her body but doesn't know
where they came from.

     3.   I have heard her call out the name "Whitey" while she's
asleep. Yet, she claims not to know who or what "Whitey" is.

     4.   Whenever Atwood talks about fishing she gets angry.
She dislikes any type of sport where killing a living creature is
involved. Yet, when I remind her that she was fishing the day
she met my husband and son, she just stares at me.

She can't answer any questions about her past. She claims she
doesn't know and that she just wants to live in the "now." If
the "now" is a place other than my garage, I'm all for it!

I look forward to any help you can give me.

Sincerely,

Polly O'Doole

Polly O'Doole

12/15/92

Dear Mrs. O'Doole :

    I received your note today concerning your interest in discovering information about a recent acquaintance. Other than suggest you ask the person to supply you with identification as you might do with anyone you took in as a "tenant," I'm at a loss how to tell you to discover someone's true identity. Of course, if you have a crime to report, your first recourse would be to contact your local police.

        Good luck.

        Sincerely,

        Tim R—

        coordinating producer

COSGROVE/MEURER PRODUCTIONS, INC.
4303 West Verdugo Avenue, Burbank, California 91505

A.J. "Honeychops" O'Doole, Founder/President
Atwood O'Doole, Senior Vice President

Polly O'Doole, Nutrition Director
Electra, Spiritual Advisor

November 4, 1992

Senator-Elect Dianne Feinstein
909 Montgomery Street, #404
San Francisco, California 94133

Dear Senator-Elect Feinstein:

My name is A.J. "Honeychops" O'Doole. Several months ago I embarked on a cross-country journey with my girlfriend to discover my life's destiny. Somewhere between Ohio and Maryland, I found it. I'm sixteen years old and I'm proud to say I've just started my own business. I manufacture and market customized capes.

I am writing to congratulate you on your election victory and applaud your success in making 1992 the "year of the woman" in politics. As a minority businessman I am inspired by your ambition in achieving something so difficult.

It is my goal to make 1993 the "year of the teenage tycoon". Do you have any advice for me as I, like yourself, try to beat the odds? While in Washington, can I count on you to help support the interests of gifted young entrepreneurs like myself?

Sincerely,

A.J. Honeychops O'Doole

A.J. "Honeychops" O'Doole

P.S. -- Someday, when my cape empire is self sufficient, I might want to be a senator myself. I think it would be neat. Would I have to go to college first?

DIANNE FEINSTEIN
CALIFORNIA

United States Senate

WASHINGTON, DC 20510-0504

January 27, 1993

Mr. A. J. O'Doole
Honeychop's House of Capes
6857 Bothwell Road
Reseda, California 91335

Dear Mr. O'Doole:

Thank you so much for your letter of November 4 offering your congratulations on my election to the United States Senate.

There is a lot to do over the next two years, and I am eager to get started on the work that lies ahead. I am looking forward to working with the Clinton Administration to end the gridlock, begin to care about people again, and solve some of the serious problems facing America.

I appreciate your kind words and thoughtfulness on this special occasion.

Sincerely,

Dianne Feinstein
United States Senator

DF:eaj

HONEYCHOPS' HOUSE OF CAPES
6857 Bothwell Rd.
Reseda, CA 91335

A.J. "Honeychops" O'Doole, Founder/President
Atwood O'Doole, Senior Vice President

Polly O'Doole, Nutrition Director
Electra, Spiritual Advisor

November 5, 1992

Universal Studios Hollywood
Mr. Jim Yeager
Director, Public Relations
100 Universal City Plaza
Bldg. SC-31
Universal City, California 91608

Dear Mr. Yeager:

My name is Atwood O'Doole. In addition to owning an awning and canopy company (O'Doole's Awning & Canopy) I am also affiliated with a groundbreaking new specialized clothing manufacturer -- Honeychops' House of Capes.

On October 31, I had the great pleasure of attending your Halloween Horror Nights celebration. Perhaps you saw me. I was wearing a minnow costume. My talented wife Polly made it for an abandoned business venture of mine. Anyway, I think it was just after I got off the earthquake ride that I had my brainstorm. How about an attraction that ties in to your blockbuster motion picture CAPE FEAR?

I see it this way -- have the tram car stop in a secluded area of the back lot. Then, twenty or thirty Robert Deniro look-alikes wearing the scariest capes you can possibly imagine, chase the guests around trying to give them religious tattoos.

The idea is yours. All I ask is that you let us make the capes for you. Also, for your information, one of our staff members here knows a bit about tattoos.

I look forward to hearing from you very soon.

Very truly yours,

Atwood O'Doole

Atwood O'Doole
Senior Vice President

January 7, 1993

Mr. Atwood O'Doole
Senior Vice President
HONEYCHOPS' HOUSE OF CAPES
6857 Bothwell Rd.
Reseda, CA 91335

Dear Mr. Atwood:

Thank you very much for you recent suggestion regarding an
attraction based on the Universal movie "Cape Fear."

Unfortunately, it's not a concept we will be able to pursue.

We're delighted you enjoyed our "Halloween Horror Nights"
celebration and hope you will visit us again this Halloween.

Thanks for thinking of Universal Studios Hollywood.

Sincerely,

Jim Yeager
Director
Public Relations

JY/sg

HONEYCHOPS' HOUSE OF CAPES

6857 Bothwell Rd.
Reseda, CA 91335

A.J. "Honeychops" O'Doole, Founder/President
Atwood O'Doole, Senior Vice President

Polly O'Doole, Nutrition Director
Electra, Spiritual Advisor

November 10, 1992

Butterball Turkey Company
2001 Butterfield Road
Downer's Grove, Illinois 60515
Attn: Consumer Communications

To Whom It May Concern:

First of all, I would like to say that I am a strict vegetarian
and would never consider consuming anything that had legs and
once walked upon the same earth as me.

However, as Thanksgiving approaches, in order to keep peace I
have to take into account the traditional customs of my fellow
earth inhabitants, specifically my boyfriend's family, no matter
how barbaric they are. While I will be dining on a meatless
menu, I cannot in all good conscience sit at the same table with
carnivors if I believe the sacrifical turkey was pained while
making its one-way trot to the dinner table.

Some Jewish people only serve kosher food. I believe this has to
do with how the animal was killed and how the food was prepared.
Although I do not adhere to the beliefs of Judaism, I respect
their respect of animals.

Are Butterball turkeys kosher? If not, what kind of spiritual
guidance is given to these animals before they are killed? I do
not want to be sitting around a table while the spirit of a
turkey who didn't "run to the light" hovers over us. It's hard
enough for me to deal with my boyfriend's mother, I don't need a
"poultrygeist" on top of it!

I look forward to hearing from you.

Light, Life and Love,

Electra

CONSUMER COMMUNICATIONS
2001 Butterfield Rd. Downers Grove, IL 60515

March 5, 1993

M. Electra
6857 Bothwell Road
Reseda, CA 91335

Dear M. Electra:

Thank you for your letter regarding Butterball Turkey.

The United States Department of Agriculture is responsible for examining the condition of animals as they are received at our plants and for ensuring that their regulations concerning the humane treatment of such animals are followed by our plants. Our company policy is to ensure that our plant operations are conducted in compliance with applicable Federal and State regulations.

We share your concern regarding the humane treatment of livestock and will continue to work with the United States Department of Agriculture to ensure that their regulations in this area are followed. We assure you that Butterball Turkey are treated humanely; however, they are not kosher.

If we can help you in any way, please feel free to contact us.

Cordially,

Tara-Rose O'Malley
Tara-Rose O'Malley
Manager

mjc

POLLY O'DOOLE
6857 BOTHWELL ROAD
RESEDA, CA 91335

November 11, 1992

Alan Dershowitz, Esq.
Harvard Law School
1525 Massachusetts Avenue
Cambridge, MA 02138

Dear Mr. Dershowitz:

I am writing to you because I know you specialize in cases that
are out of the ordinary and my family certainly qualifies for
that dubious distinction. I would appreciate it very much if you
could answer the following questions so my husband and I know how
to cope with our current dilema:

    1.   How long must two adults live together before they
qualify as "common law" husband and wife?

    2.   How long must two adults live together before one can
sue the other for "palimony?"

    3.   If the "common law" husband is under legal age and
can't be sued personally, can the "common law" wife sue his
parents for palimony?

    4.   If the "common law" husband is under legal age, can his
parents sue the "common law" wife for some form of molestation?

    5.   Is the couple considered to be living together if the
"common law" husband lives in the house with his parents and the
"common law" wife (who is more than twice the husband's age and
should know better!) is staying in the garage?

Do the answers to the above questions apply in every state or are
they different from state to state? None of these questions have
been asked or answered on Oprah or Donahue which is where I pick
up a good deal of information.

Thank you.

Polly O'Doole

Polly O'Doole

Alan M. Dershowitz   Harvard Law School
                     Cambridge, Massachusetts 02138

January 14, 1993

Ms. Polly O'Doole
6857 Bothwell Road
Reseda, CA 91335

Dear Ms. O'Doole:

     My staff has reviewed the material you sent to my of-
fice. Unfortunately, I am unable to provide you with the
answers you requested. My teaching responsibilities and
present case load prevent me from assuming any more commit-
ments.

     You may wish to seek legal counsel in California.

                    Sincerely,

                    Alan M. Dershowitz

AMD:gdm

A.J. "Honeychops" O'Doole, Founder/President
Atwood O'Doole, Senior Vice President

Polly O'Doole, Nutrition Director
Electra, Spiritual Advisor

November 11, 1992

Dr. Geraldine Morrow
American Dental Association
211 East Chicago Street
Chicago, Illinois 60611

Dear Dr. Morrow:

First of all, I want you to know that I am following your recommendation to only use ADA-approved dental floss. And please thank Suzanne Richter for her reply to my concerns about my lovely wife Polly's incessant snoring. Though I am still burdened with frequent sleepless nights, I have faith that I will eventually resolve this problem.

Now, to the reason I'm writing. My son A.J. has just started his own business making customized capes. I've volunteered to help market his services to potential clients like yourself. Most people don't realize the value of a cape. It's not just a fashion accessory. We at Honeychops' House of Capes firmly believe that capes can be fully functional. The right cape tailor made for your specific needs can be an invaluable part of your daily attire.

Have you ever given thought to a standardized dentist cape? Take a look at the enclosed sketch and let me know what you think. I want to start contacting dentists directly. But first, I'd like to get some kind of endorsement from you. I look forward to hearing from you very soon.

Very truly yours,

Atwood O'Doole

Atwood O'Doole
Senior Vice President

encl. (1 sketch -- "The O'Doole Dentist Cape")

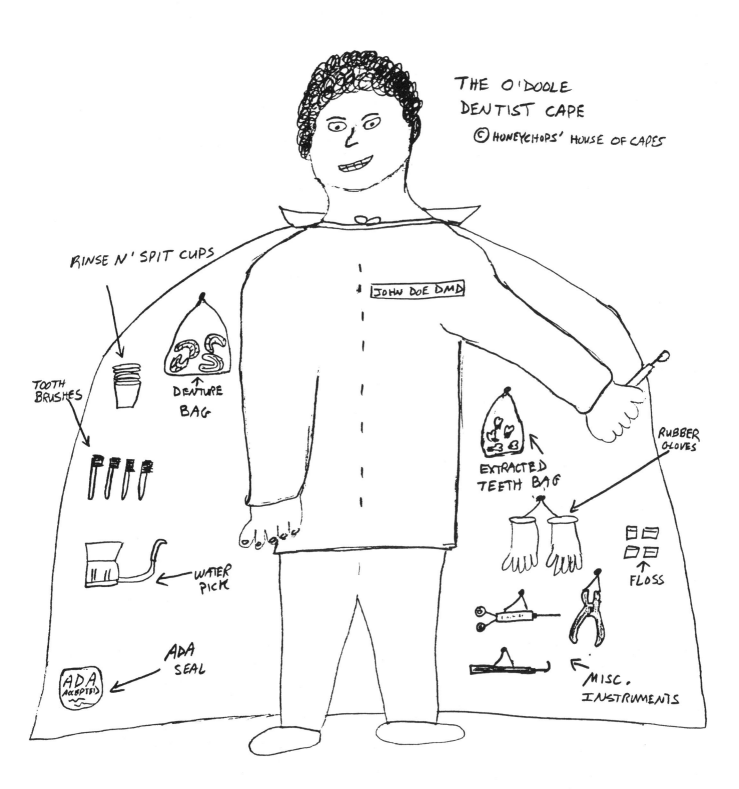

American
Dental
Association

211 East Chicago Avenue
Chicago, Illinois 60611-2678

December 2, 1992

Mr. Atwood O'Doole
6857 Bothwell Road
Reseda, CA   91335

Dear Mr. O'Doole:

I am responding to your letter to Dr. Geraldine Morrow
concerning clothing for the dental office. The Occupational
Safety and Health Administration has set specific guidelines
on the use of protective clothing for health care workers. A
cape would not meet the federal government's requirements.
Thank you for your suggestion.

Sincerely,

Nina A. Koziol
Manager, Consumer Affairs
Division of Communications

POLLY O'DOOLE
6857 BOTHWELL ROAD
RESEDA, CA 91335

November 11, 1992

Mrs. Barbara Bush
c/o The White House
1600 Pennsylvania Avenue
Washington, D.C.

Dear Mrs. Bush:

I know that during the past twelve years you have had a very busy
schedule being the First and Second Lady of the United States,
writing books, campaigning, etc. Although I imagine you'll be in
the "Grandmother" business once you leave the White House, I have
a very good idea which will pay homage to your 12 year stint in
our nation's capital. You could join Elizabeth Taylor, Estee
Lauder and Cher in the perfume business. Here's the idea:

"BARBARA BUSH'S NEW WORLD ODOR!"

Besides having an alluring fragrance, you can cash in on some of
President Bush's campaign slogans (i.e., "Barbara Bush's New
World Odor - A Kinder, Gentler Odor" or "A Very Prudent Perfume"
or how about "1000 Points of De-Light").

Please think about this. If you decide not to use it, please let
me know because I think it is too good of an idea to waste.

Sincerely,

Polly O'Doole

Polly O'Doole

P.S. Please...no secret ingredients like "Eye of Newt Gingrich!"

THE WHITE HOUSE

WASHINGTON

December 18, 1992

Dear Ms. O'Doole:

Your message to Mrs. Bush has been received.

I know Mrs. Bush would want me to convey her appreciation to you for sharing your thoughts with her.

With all best wishes,

Sincerely,

Joan C. DeCain
Director of Correspondence
for Mrs. Bush

Ms. Polly O'Doole
6857 Bothwell Road
Reseda, California   91335

Atwood O'Doole
6857 Bothwell Road
Reseda, California 91335

═══════════════════════════════

November 15, 1992

Pete Townshend
c/o Faber & Faber Ltd.
3 Queen Sq.
London, England
WC1N 3AU

Dear Pete:

    My name is Atwood O'Doole. In addition to owning my own
awning and canopy company (O'Doole's Awning and Canopy) I have a
very special reason for being a major fan of yours -- it was at a
Who concert in Kansas City in 1971 that I first met my lovely
wife Polly. We got married on December 12 of the following year.
Needless to say, the Who's music has since meant a lot to us.

    Polly is having a very difficult time these days. Our son
A.J. is dating a woman old enough to be his mother and my older
sister. I reluctantly allowed this woman to live in our garage.
Unfortunately, that's still not far enough away from Polly. You
know what they say about two women living under the same roof?
Well, it's true. There's so much tension you could cut it with a
fillet knife.

    To make things worse I've been neglecting Polly due to
spending so much time helping A.J. start a new business. But,
I'm going to make it up to her. I want our upcoming 20th Wedding
Anniversary to be extra special. Do you think you could possibly
send us some sort of Who memento like one of your guitar picks or
an autographed photo? It would mean so much to her!

    To show you how much I appreciate your bringing Polly and I
together, I've been working on something special for you at the
shop. I even named it after one of your songs. I call it The
O'Doole "Going Mobile" Awning. You'll never be rained out of a
concert again! I've enclosed a sketch. When I work out the bugs
I'll send you the real thing.

    I look forward to hearing from you very soon.

                        Very truly yours,

                        Atwood O'Doole

                        Atwood O'Doole

                        [NO RESPONSE]

POLLY O'DOOLE
6857 BOTHWELL ROAD
RESEDA, CA 91335

♥ ♥

November 18, 1992

Princess Diana
Buckingham Palace
London, England

Dear Princess Diana:

I am so sorry to hear of the unfortunate turn of affairs the royal marriage has taken. Please take some comfort in the whimsical lyrics of the enclosed song I have written entitled "I'm Gamblin' With My Life Staying Married to You."

Also bear in mind that, for generations, millions of women all over the globe have endured the misery of being trapped in a loveless marriage. I, thank God, have no first-hand knowledge of this because my husband, Atwood, has always treated me like a queen. He's kind, generous, ambitious, loving and good with our children and pets. If I had to complain, I guess I'd say that sometimes I think he loves going fishing more than he loves me. However, he bears a striking resemblence to Clint Eastwood and since he doesn't insist I accompany him on his fishing trips, I think I'm ahead of the game!

Take solace in the fact that you are young and beautiful with an exciting life ahead of you while the most obvious thing Camilla has in common with your husband is that they look alike!

Please give Prince Charles a kiss for me. Maybe he'll turn back into the frog we all know he is for mistreating you. Better yet, here's an order form for some lipstick that lasts 24 hours. Give him a few great big kisses on the cheek when he leaves in the morning. It will be invisible at first. He'll be embarassed all day long, plus you get to yell at him later for being a two-timer!

Sincerely,

Polly O'Doole

Polly O'Doole

I'M GAMBLIN' WITH MY LIFE STAYING MARRIED TO YOU
by Polly O'Doole

I'm goin' out to play Bingo by myself
I'm goin' out to play Bingo by myself
If I win some cash on "G-52"
That's enough cash for me to leave you
I'm goin' to out play Bingo by myself

I'm buyin' lotto tickets just for me
I'm buyin' lotto tickets just for me
If all my numbers do come in
I'll be gone 'fore you drink a pint of gin
I'm buyin' lotto tickets just for me

I'm spendin' coupon savings in a poker game
I'm spendin' coupon savings in a poker game
If the Lord gives me a royal flush
I'll unload you, you big old lush
I'm spendin' coupon savings in a poker game

I'm investin' grocery money in the Sweepstakes
I'm investin' grocery money in the Sweepstakes
I'd rather live on water and gruel
Than stay married to a two-timin' fool
I'm investin' grocery money in the Sweepstakes

I'm goin' to the racetrack with our rent
I'm goin' to the racetrack with our rent
If the daily double comes in for me
I'll leave you and your freeloadin' family
I'm goin' to the racetrack with our rent

I'm gamblin' with my life staying married to you
I'm gamblin' with my life staying married to you
I should've listened to my mother
And stayed single after divorcing your brother
I'm gamblin' with my life staying married to you

ST. JAMES'S PALACE
LONDON SW1A 1BS

2nd December 1992

Dear Mrs O'Toole,

The Princess of Wales has asked me to
thank you for your letter.

Her Royal Highness much appreciated your
kind words and has asked me to send you her
very best wishes.

Yours sincerely,

Jean Lee.

Lady-in-Waiting

A.J. "Honeychops" O'Doole, Founder/President
Atwood O'Doole, Senior Vice President

Polly O'Doole, Nutrition Director
Electra, Spiritual Advisor

November 18, 1992

Willard Scott
c/o "THE TODAY SHOW"
NBC
30 Rockefeller Plaza
New York, NY 10112

Dear Willard:

My name is Atwood O'Doole. In addition to owning my own awning and canopy company ("O'Doole's Awning & Canopy") I also watch The Today Show every morning while eating my corn flakes. I think you're the greatest weatherman on tv. Besides having to get up so early and having to work with Bryant, I bet this is the best job you've ever had. Speaking of your co-workers, is Katie Couric as cute and perky in person? Please tell her I've still got her photo hanging in my shop.

Willard, you proved you were a maverick broadcaster several years ago when you did the weather dressed as Carmen Miranda. Don't you think that now, with your show trailing Good Morning America, that it's time to get noticed again? It has recently come to my attention that no one on network television wears a cape. I think it would be a most bold and profitable move if you became the first. I've been working on something for you here at the House of Capes. Please examine the enclosed sketch and let me know what you think. I'd make it for you for free if you'd just give us a plug one morning.

And one more thing -- do you have to be real old to have your birthday or anniversary mentioned on your show? If not, maybe you could say something about my lovely wife Polly and I having our 20th Wedding Anniversary on December 12th.

I anxiously await your reply.

Very truly yours,

Atwood O'Doole

Atwood O'Doole
Senior Vice President

encl. -- (1 sketch -- "The O'Doole Weatherman Cape")

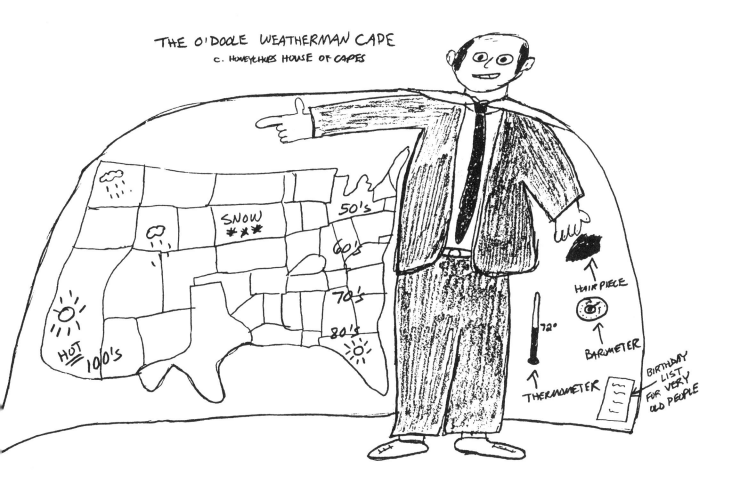

THE O'DOOLE WEATHERMAN CAPE
c. HONEYCHURS HOUSE OF CAPES

SNOW
***

50's

60's

70's

80's

HOT 100's

72°

HAIR PIECE

BAROMETER

THERMOMETER

BIRTHDAY LIST FOR VERY OLD PEOPLE

January 5, 1993

Atwood O'Doole
Senior Vice President
Honeychops' House of Capes
6857 Bothwell Road
Reseda, California 91335

Dear Mr. O'Doole,

Thank you for your letter and offer of the
cape. Inasmuch as Batman and I are similar
in physique, I fear I might be mistaken for
him.

Give my love to your wife Polly and I hope
your 20th Anniversary was a great occasion.
May you have at least 50 more (55 if I am to
announce it).

Best wishes for success and happiness in 1993
and always.

Willard Scott

HONEYCHOPS' HOUSE OF CAPES
6857 Bothwell Rd.
Reseda, CA 91335

A.J. "Honeychops" O'Doole, Founder/President
Atwood O'Doole, Senior Vice President

Polly O'Doole, Nutrition Director
Electra, Spiritual Advisor

November 19, 1992

NASA
PA-EAB
John F. Kennedy Space Center
Cape Canaveral, Florida 32899

Dear Sir/Madame:

My name is A.J. "Honeychops" O'Doole. In addition to being sixteen
years old and owning my own cape manufacturing company ("Honeychops'
House of Capes") I am also fascinated with space travel. For a
while I wanted to be an astronaut. And I might still do it someday.
Even though I heard you had to go to college for a long time. Could
you tell me the best school to go to?

When I watch the blast offs from Cape Canaveral on tv I never see
people wearing capes. I think it would be neet for you to sell
capes in your gift shop. And what about those astronaut uniforms?
They look like they've been pretty much the same for years. Do you
have any plans to change them? If so, what would you think about
adding a cape? We can make capes with lots of pockets so you could
carry more moon rocks. How much do moon rocks weigh anyway? More
than bricks? We'd need to know that.

I look forward to hearing from you really soon.

Sincerely,

A.J. "Honeychops" O'Doole

A.J. "Honeychops" O'Doole

P.S. -- How come Captain Kirk and the crew never wear space suits
when they're on other planets?

HONEYCHOPS' HOUSE OF CAPES
6857 Bothwell Rd.
Reseda, CA 91335

A.J. "Honeychops" O'Doole, Founder/President
Atwood O'Doole, Senior Vice President

Polly O'Doole, Nutrition Director
Electra, Spiritual Advisor

November 19, 1992

NASA
PA-EAB
John F. Kennedy Space Center
Cape Canaveral, Florida 32899

Dear Sir/Madame:

My name is A.J. "Honeychops" O'Doole. In addition to being sixteen
years old and owning my own cape manufacturing company ("Honeychops'
House of Capes") I am also fascinated with space travel. For a
while I wanted to be an astronaut. And I might still do it someday.
Even though I heard you had to go to college for a long time. Could
you tell me the best school to go to?

When I watch the blast offs from Cape Canaveral on tv I never see
people wearing capes. I think it would be neet for you to sell
capes in your gift shop. And what about those astronaut uniforms?
They look like they've been pretty much the same for years. Do you
have any plans to change them? If so, what would you think about
adding a cape? We can make capes with lots of pockets so you could
carry more moon rocks. How much do moon rocks weigh anyway? More
than bricks? We'd need to know that.

I look forward to hearing from you really soon.

Sincerely,

A.J. "Honeychops" O'Doole

A.J. "Honeychops" O'Doole

P.S. -- How come Captain Kirk and the crew never wear space suits
when they're on other planets? *Because that would hide
their faces, I think!*

*Capes would float freely
in microgravity and be
very much in the way.
Enjoy the enclosed materials.*

*Joseph Green
KSC Education Office*

NASA

National Aeronautics and
Space Administration

Information Summaries

PMS 017-C (KSC)
September 1991

Living and Working
on the New Frontier

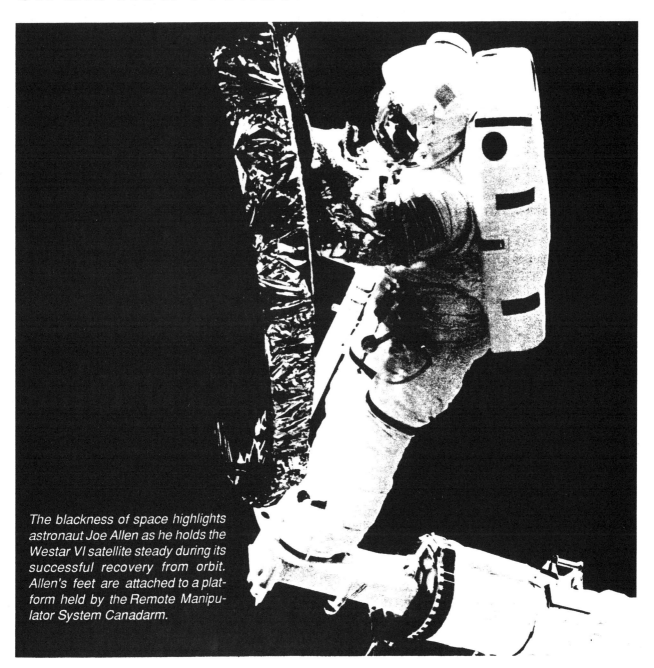

The blackness of space highlights astronaut Joe Allen as he holds the Westar VI satellite steady during its successful recovery from orbit. Allen's feet are attached to a platform held by the Remote Manipulator System Canadarm.

Things are starting to get interesting around here. I stumbled across this missing person ad in the Pennysaver. Although A.J.'s girlfriend's name is "Electra," I can't help but think she's a ringer for one "Eloise" from "Cle Elum." To tell you the truth, I thought her attraction to A.J. was pretty fishy from the start. Now the picture is starting to get clearer. She's probably on the lam and used my brother for her getaway driver. What if she's an ax-murderer? If she is then I can hack up Mom's guitar and blame it on her. I've decided not to discuss this with anyone until I have more information. So, Dear Diary, mum's the word!

MO

Atwood O'Doole
6857 Bothwell Road
Reseda, California 91335

═══════════════════════════════

November 27, 1992

Kate Hutton, PhD
California Institute of Technology
Seismological Laboratory 252-21
Pasadena, California 91125

Dear Dr. Hutton:

My name is Atwood O'Doole. In addition to owning my own
awning and canopy company (O'Doole's Awning & Canopy) I am also a
southern California home owner. This morning I was shaken out of
bed at 8:00 am, as were many Los Angelites, by what I've since
heard was a 5.4 earthquake. Having weathered many such temblors,
I am quite familiar with the structural damage they can cause my
humble abode. Normally, I notice vertical cracks in the walls.
But this time I was surprised to see various winding cracks
which, perhaps coincidentally or perhaps not, form the image of
my son A.J.'s girlfriend, Electra.

Electra and my lovely wife Polly do not get along. In fact,
yesterday (Thanksgiving Day) they had quite a skirmish in our
kitchen. It seems that the oven was "inadvertently" set at 500
degrees, turning our turkey into a small lump of coal. Polly,
who is a professional cook, refused to take blame for the
incident. As a result, she became violent. I was in the garage
making doll flies when I heard banging on the walls. A.J. and I
immediately broke the fight up and separated the women. We ended
up having Electra's bean sprout casserole and herb tea for
dinner.

I didn't notice the cracks until this morning, after the
quake. Polly rigidly claims that nature is solely responsible
for the damage, but I'm just not sure. For insurance purposes
and my own peace of mind, I'm going to have to know. So maybe
you can help. In post World War II homes, is damage from
earthquakes limited to vertical cracks near support areas or
could they also result in crater-like depressions which could
possibly resemble the outline of a human being?

Very truly yours,

Atwood O'Doole

Atwood O'Doole

CALIFORNIA INSTITUTE OF TECHNOLOGY

December 9, 1992

Atwood O'Doole
6857 Bothwell Road
Reseda CA 91335

Dear Mr. O'Doole,

It's hard for me to tell from your description, but it doesn't really sound like earthquake damage. Mild earthquake damage generally shows itself as diagonal cracking around windows and doors in plaster or stucco or, in the case of drywall, the panels may separate along vertical cracks. Deformation of a wall would only result if, for example, the house slid off the foundation, or if "something" crashed into it.

On the other hand, it's hard for me to imagine Electra doing that much damage to a wall without doing equal damage to herself!

You might care to have an engineer look at the wall, if there is an insurance claim involved. You could also look at examples in books like _Peace_of_Mind_in_Earthquake_Country_ by Peter Yanev.

I have to say that this is one of the more unusual requests for information that I have ever gotten!

Kate Hutton
Staff Seismologist

Kate Hutton

Atwood O'Doole
6857 Bothwell Road
Reseda, California 91335

==

November 30, 1992

Bass Pro Shops
1935 S. Campbell
Springfield, MO 65898-0001

Dear Sir/Madame:

     My name is Atwood O'Doole. In addition to owning my own
awning and canopy company ("O'Doole's Awning & Canopy") I am also
one of your many satisfied customers. My garage used to be
chocked full of your many high quality rods and reels, soft
tackle items and crank baits. Unfortunately, since allowing my
son A.J.'s girlfriend to reside in my garage in September, I
can't locate many of my most beloved fishing accessories. I've
got a sneaking suspicion she's responsible.

     I'm about at my wits end with her. I used to consider the
garage as my own private getaway where I could escape for a while
from the daily pressures of being a father, husband and self-
employed businessman. A place where I could tinker, ponder and
dream to my heart's content. Now, this woman has filled my
personal space with lava lamps, strobe lights, peace signs and a
smelly incense which is starting to give me a migraine headache.

     You probably can't offer much help with my unwanted house
guest dilemma, but, considering our recessionary times, perhaps
you could give me a special deal to replace all the stuff this
insenstive woman has thrown out. I added up everything that's
missing, including my Stealth 300 Trolling Motor. It'd cost me
$400 and change to replace it all. What do you say? Can you
give me a break? How about $300?

     One more thing. I've been dropping hints to the kids for
months now about how I'd like a Tripple Ripple Protein Worm Kit
for Christmas. Have they placed an order with you yet? If you
tell me I promise I won't tell them I know.

                              Very truly yours,

                              Atwood O'Doole
                              Atwood O'Doole

Bass Pro Shops
SPRINGFIELD MO

BASS PRO SHOPS
1935 South Campbell
Springfield, MO 65898

From the Desk of:

DOLORES DAVIS

Customer Service Representative

TO: Atwood O'Drole
18517 Bothwell Rd
Reseda, Ca
91335

DATE: 12-11-92

ORDER #: _____

Please excuse my informality. In order that I can serve you promptly, I have taken the liberty of replying with this note.

I'm sorry, but we will be unable to give you a price cut on your order. Our prices are already at their lowest price. I have added you to our mailing list so you will be receiving our seasonal free catalogs.

Thank you
Dolores

P.S. Please direct your reply to my attention.

83-13051

HONEYCHOPS' HOUSE OF CAPES

6857 Bothwell Rd.

Reseda, CA 91335

A.J. "Honeychops" O'Doole, Founder/President   Polly O'Doole, Nutrition Director
Atwood O'Doole, Senior Vice President   Electra, Spiritual Advisor

December 1, 1992

Mr. Ken A. Wherry
Sr. Vice President, Operations
Eddie Bauer, Inc.
15010 N.E. 36th Street
Redmond, Washington 98052

Dear Mr. Wherry:

A lot has happened since you wrote me back in May. I met a girl.
I travelled the country. I got a new name. I won some money in
Atlantic City. And I discovered my destiny -- to manufacture
customized capes.

Owning my own business is neet but it's a lot harder than I thought
it would be. Especially since I'm still in school and have a lot
of Algebra II homework. Fortunately, my dad has been helping me a
lot. I don't know what I'd do without him. I took your advice and
stepped back for a different look at why he was urging me to take
over his business. I finally realized that his actions weren't
selfish. He just wanted me to do well and carry on the O'Doole
name. He's actually very un-selfish. He told me he hopes my cape
business will be more successful than his awning and canopy company.

The only problem I have now is the ongoing feud between my
girlfriend, Electra, and my mom. They had a big fight on
Thanksgiving Day and Mom ended up burning the turkey. She doesn't
think Electra is the right girl for me. She'd rather I date
somebody more traditional like Laura Ingalls on "Little House on the
Prairie". From what you told me, Eddie Bauer had some stress at
home too. So, maybe all this will actually help me.

In browsing through your catalogue I realized that you don't make
capes. Why not? They're going to be really popular. How would you
like to sell my capes? I'd make you a real good deal. Let me know
right away because I'm going to talk to other people too.

Sincerely,

A.J. Honeychops O'Doole

A.J. "Honeychops" O'Doole

encl. -- one "Honeychops' House of Capes" pencil

EDDIE BAUER, INC.
15010 N.E. 36th Street
Redmond, Washington 98052

January 21, 1993

Mr. A.J. O'Doole
Honeychops' House of Capes
6857 Bothwell Road
Preseda, CA 91336

Dear A.J.:

I did receive your letter dated December 1, 1992, but only three days prior to your sending me the copy on January 4, 1993 with your note. It had gone to two other departments and I'm not sure why, but I apologize for not getting back to you earlier.

Eddie Bauer was in the cape business for four years, not only in our Catalogs but in our Retail stores. Enclosed are two photo copies of the Catalog presentations which were in 4-color and quite well done.

Original response to the introduction to capes was enthusiastic to the point that we added a plaid to the original loden green, giving our customers a choice. Original catalog photos attracted interest by using, as props, two leopards borrowed from a taxidermist of our acquaintance. This perhaps helped sales, but what we did receive was a deluge of letters from animal lovers protesting our "exploiting an endangered species." In subsequent appearances we eliminated the leopards and concentrated on the capes with no appreciable gain in revenue.

In-person interviews with our customers who had purchased the capes were singularly disappointing, result-wise. In substance, lack of enthusiasm was two-fold: not warm or protective enough for inclement weather and "the cape can't be worn with just anything, such as a down jacket, but must be teamed with a complimentary ensemble."

Therefore, based on our past experience I must decline, with thanks, your offer to sell your capes.

Sincere best wishes for every success in your future business endeavors.

Cordially,

Ken

Ken Wherry

KW/kac
cust/memo16

100% Virgin Wool
CONTINENTAL CAPES

Styling is a timeless classic, unchanged in functional ingenuity since first worn by Her Royal Majesty at Austerlitz in 1726.

This smartly fashionable imported cape will keep your Lady cozy warm and enviably chic for shopping sprees in the village plaza, country club bazaars, field trials and sports car rallies.

Enviably adaptable to accessories and situations; converts instantly from full cape drape to self-sleeve styling.

Tailoring is meticulous in the Old Country tradition. Fabric is 100% Virgin Wool, closely woven and felted to repel wind and weather.

Sizes: S/M/L.

Color: Loden Green.

No. 1210..ppd. **$49.50** ③•

22

Atwood O'Doole
6857 Bothwell Road
Reseda, California 91335

December 4, 1992

Ripley's Believe it Or Not
Attn: Norm Deska, Vice President
90 Elington Avenue, Suite 510
Toronto, Ontario
Canada M4P2Y3

Dear Mr. Deska:

My name is Atwood O'Doole. In addition to owning my own awning and canopy company ("O'Doole's Awning & Canopy") I am an average American citizen who rarely witnesses anything out of the ordinary. Until now.

Last night at around 9:20 pm we had another in a series of recent earthquakes. I was watching CHEERS with my lovely wife Polly when it happened. She asked me if we should go check on the kids, who were in their rooms, or on Electra, my son A.J.'s girlfriend, who was in the garage. I just stared at her and didn't say anything. I was too engrossed in my favorite sitcom to be concerned with the well being of others. And, I didn't think the tremor was big enough to cause any harm. I was wrong.

A few minutes later Electra came into the den. "Who am I and why am I here?" she asked in an uncharacteristically dainty tone. She wanted to know why she was wearing tie-dye clothes and had the word "Honeychops" tatooed over her heart. We reminded her of how she kidnapped A.J., traipsed around the country in my van and came back to help him start his own cape company. She couldn't remember any of it. She said her name was Eloise Dibble and she was from Cle Elum, Washington. The last thing she remembered was being hit on the head with a softball while walking to Glondo's Sausage Company for some beef jerky.

In the garage, I found my snore box (an original invention of mine) in the floor next to Electra's sleeping bag. It had fallen off a shelf during the earthquake and hit her on the head. As a result, she got her memory back. It's an amazing story. A sweet, innocent woman lost her memory and assumed the identity of a middle aged gypsy woman -- for nearly six months. It's <u>hard to believe</u>, but it's true! Would you like to use this story in one of your books or museums? Please let me know right away. I'm going to talk to the Guiness people too.

I anxiously await your reply.

Very truly yours,

Atwood O'Doole
Atwood O'Doole

Ripley's Believe It or Not!®

EXECUTIVE OFFICES

90 Eglinton Avenue East

Suite 510

Toronto, Ontario,

Canada M4P 2Y3

January 13, 1993

Mr. Atwood O'Doole
6857 Bothwell Road
Reseda, California
U.S.A.
91335

Dear Mr. O'Doole,

Thank you for your recent letter. Your account of Electra's strange accident is indeed quite unbelievable. If the story can be verified by witnesses, including Electra and her family, Ripley's would indeed be interested in publishing this story.

Mr. O'Doole, if you would like to see this story published, please provide us with photos, news clippings, testimonies and sworn affidavits from all those involved and we will have our research staff review this story for possible future publication.

Mr. O'Doole, we appreciate your interest in Ripley's Believe It or Not! and look forward to hearing from you soon.

Yours truly,

RIPLEY'S BELIEVE IT OR NOT!

Edward T. Meyer
Vice President
Exhibits & Archives

ETM/lb

Ripley's Believe It or Not!
Pty. Limited

Ripley's Attractions Inc.

Ripley Entertainment Inc.

Louis Tussaud's Wax Museum
(Blackpool) A/S

Jim Pattison
Industries Limited

Jim Pattison U.S.A. Inc.

Robert Ripley 1935

A.J. "Honeychops" O'Doole, Founder/President
Atwood O'Doole, Senior Vice President

Polly O'Doole, Nutrition Director
~~Electra, Spiritual Advisor~~

December 8, 1992

Tom Petty
P.O. Box 532
Encino, California 91426-0532

Dear Tom:

My name is A.J. "Honeychops" O'Doole. I'm sixteen years old and I'm really bummed out now. I've been listening to your song "FREE FALLING" over and over and over again. I can really relate to it being a "long day livin' in Reseda" with a "free-way runnin' through the yard". You see, I just lost my girlfriend. I didn't break her heart like the guy in your song though. She didn't dump me either. It's pretty bizarre but the truth is -- ever since I started dating her she had amnesia and was actually somebody else. Now she's gone home to to her husband and two kids.

It probably wouldn't have worked out anyway since she's nearly thirty years older than me. But still, it hurts. And I've got problems with my business ("Honeychops' House of Capes") too. My dad has been helping me a lot with marketing and stuff but he's got to start spending more time with his awning and canopy company ("O'Doole's Awning & Canopy"). And I don't think I can run a business by myself and still get all my homework done.

My mom writes songs and she says the best ones are the ones she wrote when she was really down and out. I'm kind of thinking about writing a song or two myself. I noticed that you collaborate a lot with people. Would you like to collaborate with me? Please let me know right away. We'd need to get to work before I start feeling better.

Sincerely,

A.J. "Honeychops" O'Doole

A.J. "Honeychops" O'Doole

Tom Petty & the Heartbreakers
P.O. Box 260159
Encino, CA 91426-9998

Address Correction Requested

Hello!

long Time No SEE
BEEN busy on NEW
TRACKS. good News is
T.P. & H.B's GREATEST Hits
will be in your LOCAL STORES
by THANKSGIVING (includes 2 New
Songs) "MARY JANES LAST DANCE"
& "Something in the Air"
See ya in '94 with NEW solo
L.P. LOTSA LOVE T.P.

A.J. O'DOOLE
HONEYCHOPS HOUSE OF CAPES
6857 BOTHWELL RD.
RESEDA, CA
          91335

O'DOOLE & SON'S AWNINGS, CANOPIES AND CAPES
6857 Bothwell Rd.
Reseda, CA 91335

Atwood O'Doole, Owner   A.J. "Honeychops" O'Doole, Heir

December 12, 1992

Mr. Peter Dekom, Esq.
Bloom, Dekom & Hergott
150 South Rodeo Drive
Beverly Hills, California 90212

Dear Peter:

It's been a while since I've written. A lot has happened. I think
I've probably aged five years in the last year. And I'm much
happier. I owe a lot of it to you for challenging me to "lead
myself along a path to self-discovery by following my own clues".
The path led me all over the country and right back to 6857 Bothwell
Road, home sweet home.

I got a copy of the Bill of Rights. You were right about it giving
me the freedom to choose my own destiny. I chose to run my own cape
manufacturing company ("Honeychops' House of Capes"). After a
while, I realized it was too much for me to handle so I merged my
company with my dad's ("O'Doole's Awning & Canopy"). We haven't
done the paperwork yet. Do you think you could help us?

I told my dad about you and how you inspired me to find myself. I
asked him if we could make a cape for you. He thought it was a neet
idea. We're working on it right now. I've enclosed a drawing dad
did. We'll send the cape to you when it's finished. What color
would you like it to be? Are there enough pockets?

Sincerely,

A.J. "Honeychops" O'Doole

A.J. "Honeychops" O'Doole

encl. -- (1 sketch -- "The O'Doole Lawyer Cape"
            1 free pencil)

THE O'DOOLE LAWYER CAPE

C. O'DOOLE AND SON'S AWNINGS, CANOPIES AND CAPES

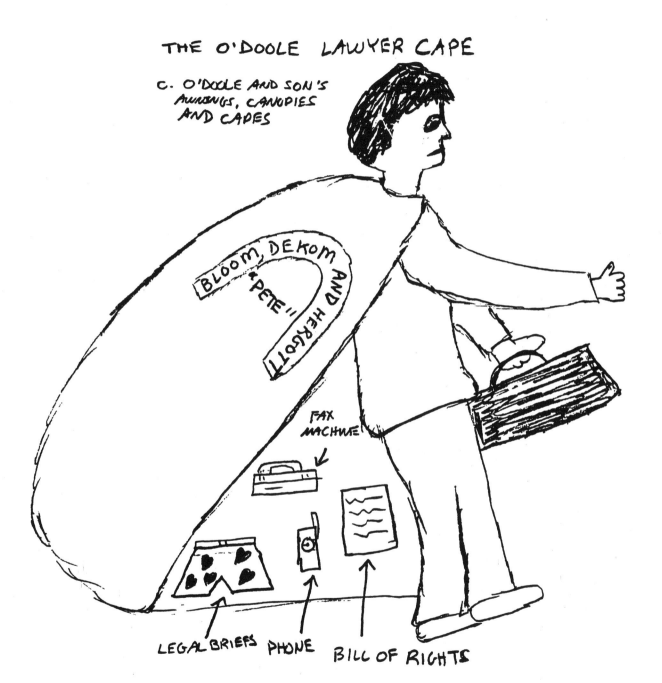

BLOOM, DEKOM AND HERZOTT & PETE

FAX MACHINE

LEGAL BRIEFS   PHONE   BILL OF RIGHTS

BLOOM, DEKOM AND HERGOTT

ATTORNEYS AT LAW

JACOB A. BLOOM   GARY L. GILBERT
PETER J. DEKOM   STUART M. ROSENTHAL
ALAN S. HERGOTT   LEIGH BRECHEEN
LAWRENCE H. GREAVES   STEPHEN F. BREIMER
CANDICE S. HANSON   DEBORAH L. KLEIN
MELANIE COOK   JONATHAN BLAUFARB
TINA J. KAHN   STEVEN L. BROOKMAN
JULIE M. PHILIPS   LARY SIMPSON
THOMAS F. HUNTER   JOHN LaVIOLETTE
JOHN D. DIEMER   ROBYN L. ROTH
STEPHEN D. BARNES

150 SOUTH RODEO DRIVE, THIRD FLOOR
BEVERLY HILLS, CALIFORNIA 90212

THOMAS P. POLLOCK
FOUNDING PARTNER
THROUGH 1986

December 15, 1992

A.J. "Honeychops" O'Doole
6857 Bothwell Rd.
Reseda, CA 91335

Dear "Honeychops":

    It finally awned on me that by giving you advice, I may
have opened a can o' peas. Maybe you should think about writing
caper pictures. Happy holidays.

                              Very truly yours,

                              PETER J. DEKOM
                              of BLOOM, DEKOM and HERGOTT

PJD/bfb

Season's Greetings

Dear Friends, Family, Neighbors: Christmas 1992

As the Christmas Season once again approaches, the O'Doole clan thought it might be fun to put our yearly news letter to the tune of one of our favorite Christmas Carols, "Jingle Bells." Of course, those of you who are really close already know about the missing person reports, stolen vehicles and the joys of entrepreneurship.

"Jingle Bells"
lyrics by A.J., Atwood and Polly O'Doole

Verse 1	Verse 2	Chorus

A.J.:

Dashing to and fro / *She taught me lots of things* / *Jingle Bells*
in my father's stolen van / *She explained the Zodiac* / *A.J. Sells*
I drove East then Westward Ho / *But she had amnesia the whole time!* / *Custom designed capes*
With a vegetarian / *Now she's gone and won't be back!* / *Oh what fun! and they're homespun*
Out of dacron, wools and crepes

Thank you Mom
Thank you Dad
You let me take life's journey
Next time I get in a jam
I'll call my new attorney!

ATWOOD:

Last May my son and I / *Instead of getting mad* / *Jingle Bells*
Went North on a vacation / *I simply hitched back home* / *Mackerels*
Our plans went quite awry / *And hit the roof when I found out* / *Blue Fish, Cod and Perch*
When he stole my transportation / *That nobody was home!* / *When I fish I'm close to God*
That's why I don't go to church

Polly's food
Is her livelihood
I don't think she should linger
On the thought that one day soon
She'll be a famous singer!

POLLY:

My husband likes to fish / *I work all day at school* / *This O'Doole*
He likes the great outdoors / *It's food I'm always slinging* / *Wishes You'll*
He also invents gadgets / *But this O'Doole does dream* / *Have Good Holidays*
to suppress my snores! / *Of country western singing!* / *Come and visit often*
But please don't plan to stay

When in town
Please jot down
hotel numbers and names
Ever since our last houseguest
The O'Dooles just aren't the same!

May God bless you and keep you in good health!

Thank you for remembering us during the Yuletide Season. We deeply appreciate your kindness in sharing the joy of the holidays with us. We join in sending best wishes to you and yours for health and happiness in the New Year.

Gg Bush　　　*Barbara Bush*

THE WHITE HOUSE
WASHINGTON

29 USA

Mr. Polly O'Dolle
6857 Bothwell Road
Reseda, California　91335

Ms. Polly O'Doole
6857 Bothwell Road
Reseda, CA 91335

Hillary Rodham Clinton

Thanks for your encouragement and support. Bill and I appreciate your help as he implements his agenda for change in America.

Best wishes, Hillary

JAMES STEWART

Dear Polly:

Thank you for your welcome holiday
letter.

Mr. Stewart was very pleased to hear
from you at Christmas time.

Your news letter was very charming
and much appreciated.   Thank you.

Mr. Stewart sends you all every good
wish for a great 1993 and a wonderful
life.

Sincerely,

Claire Priest

Claire Priest
secretary

J S
P. O. BOX 90
BEVERLY HILLS, CA 90213

Polly O'Doole

6857 Bothwell Road

Reseda, CA 91335